CANYON KILLERS

CANYON KILLERS

BRADFORD SCOTT

CUTTING EDGE

ISBN-13: 978-1-957868-28-8

Published by
Cutting Edge Books
PO Box 8212
Calabasas, CA 91372
www.cuttingedgebooks.com

CHAPTER ONE

"**S**HADOW, WHAT IN BLAZES are those jiggers down there up to, anyhow?"

Sitting his great black horse in the shadow of a cliff, Ranger Walt Slade watched with interest the activities of several men moving about in the brush that fringed the rimrock of Skull Canyon some six hundred yards farther down the rock strewn slope. Slade counted five of them altogether. A little farther back five horses were tethered in the growth.

The men seemed absorbed in the canyon below which lay silent and deserted, checkered by the gold and the shadows of the late sunshine. Their interest appeared to lie somewhere in the south, for they gesticulated in that direction and seemed to be discussing something.

From the elevation where he sat, Slade could view the canyon to where it wound around a cliff bulge and could follow its south-ward trend for more than a mile beyond the bulge. He glanced about at his more immediate surroundings.

To the right the slope tumbled down into a second and nar-rower canyon set almost at right angles to Skull Canyon. It was a box and its end wall was the rimrock wall of Skull Canyon. Where Slade sat his horse a faint trail coming up from the south curved around the cliff face, following a bench that rambled on into the north. Slade had reached Skull Canyon by way of that old trail from the south, having gathered that by way of Skull he could reach the cow town of Lucas, the county seat that had in a way taken the place of old Tascosa as the cowboy capital of the Texas Panhandle plains.

Slade returned his gaze to the group on the rimrock. He considered their actions a bit suspicious, to put it mildly. They had taken up positions on the lip of the wall, each behind a sheltering clump of brush, and were gazing steadily south. Slade could see the gleam of shifted rifle barrels. His long gray eyes, set beneath heavy black brows, narrowed a trifle. The brows drew together until there was a deep concentration furrow between. Those long eyes were usually filled with little dancing lights of laughter, but now there was no laughter in them and they were coldly gray as the rimrock.

Slade made a striking picture against the pale stone of the cliff. Very tall, much more than six feet, the breadth of his shoulders and the depth of his chest were in proportion to his height. His face was deeply bronzed, his cheeks lean, his nose strongly curved. Above his square chin and powerful jaw his rather wide mouth, normally grin-quirked at the corners, was firm-lipped but kindly. He wore the careless garb of the rangeland—faded overalls and soft blue shirt with a vivid neckerchief looped at the throat, batwing chaps and high-heeled half-boots of softly tanned leather. Double cartridge belts encircled his sinewy waist and from the plain black butts of the heavy guns protruding from carefully worked and oiled cut-out holsters his slender hands seemed never far away. Under the pushed-back, broad-brimmed "J.B." his hair showed crisp and black.

The men on the rimrock assumed an air of expectancy. Slade could see them fingering their rifles. Instinctively his own hand dropped to the butt of the heavy Winchester snugged in the saddle boot beneath his left thigh.

For minutes nothing happened. Then a yellow shimmer began boiling up against the southern sky. Slade watched it with interest, saw it thicken and roll nearer. A few minutes more and a multitude of bouncing shapes came into view.

The hurrying shapes resolved into cattle, two hundred head or more and travelling fast. Too dang fast, Slade decided. Only somebody lacking either brains or good intentions would shove a herd along like that. He felt that something was very much wrong. A stolen herd? Perhaps. With the men on the rimrock waiting to intercept it and shoot it out with the thieves? That, too, could well be possible. A very interested spectator, he watched for the drama to unfold.

However, nothing dramatic occurred. The men on the rimrock were standing up, making no effort at concealment. They were watching the progress of the approaching herd with what appeared to be but casual interest. As it swept around the bulge a couple of hundred yards to the south they strolled forward, peering down into the canyon. One raised his hand and waved it. Slade saw the flicker of an answering wave from a half dozen cowhands, at least they were dressed like cowhands, who were shoving the herd along.

Quickly the herd was past and churning northward. Another moment and it was out of sight. The men on the rimrock strolled back to their places of concealment and to all appearances comfortably relaxed. Now and then one would rise and glance to the south, then resume his squat in the brush.

Very much intrigued and more than a little puzzled, Slade stayed right where he was. He had a premonition that things were a long ways from what they should be. What was in the wind he had not the slightest notion, but he resolved to stick around till he found out what it was.

For nearly an hour nothing happened. Then the silent watcher on the hill again saw the yellow shimmer foam up against the southern sky. It was smaller, thinner this time, and travelled much more swiftly.

The dust cloud spread out, individual particles dancing like flecks of fire in the sunlight; under it Slade could see movement. A breath of wind apparently beat against the yellow haze, whisked it away like a curtain. With startling abruptness half a dozen horsemen bulged into view as if materializing from thin air, and they were coming at top speed. Slade saw the group on the rimrock alert; he caught the gleam of raised rifles.

Slade was getting what appeared to be the drift of things now. The men shoving the herd along were wideloopers, those charging up from the south a sheriff's posse hot on their trail. The bunch on the rimrock? Slade didn't know for sure, but those raised rifles looked ominous. And the barrels were trained on the advancing horsemen. He resolved to take a hand. If he was wrong, explanations would be in order. If he was right he'd be doing a good chore from a peace officer's point of view. He decided on an expedient that should get results but still leave him in the clear if he was making a mistake. He slid the Winchester from the boot and clamped the butt against his shoulder. His eyes glanced along the sights.

The report rang out like thunder in the silence, sending a thousand echoes flying from the cliffs. The men on the rimrock ducked and yelped as the slug screamed over their heads. Again and again Slade fired, clipping twigs from the growth, kicking up spurts of dust on either side of the scrambling group. A wild volley answered him, but he was invisible in the shadow and no bullets came close. He shifted the rifle muzzle a little and dropped the big slugs a trifle lower, as if he were getting the range.

Evidently that was how the bunch of apparent drygulchers on the rimrock figured it; there was a concerted rush for the horses that were snorting and lunging in the growth. An instant later all five went careening into the depths of the side canyon with lead still whining over their heads. Slade saw the spray fly in a silver shower as the horses plunged into the stream and floundered across, half running, half swimming, for evidently the water was rather deep. Up the far bank they clambered and crashed into the brush and out of sight. Slade began shoving fresh cartridges into the magazine of his rifle and his face was grim. There was no longer any doubt in his mind but the group had been up to no good. Quite likely they were in cahoots with the bunch shoving the cattle through Skull Canyon and had been stationed on the rimrock to discourage any attempt at pursuit. And the purposeful way in which they handled their rifles hinted at murder, nothing less.

"I expect it would have been better if we'd stopped as many of them as we could," he told Shadow, "but dang it! you can't go throwing lead promiscuously at people just because you're suspicious as to their intentions. Anyhow it looks like we've run into an interesting side angle that could be connected with the chore that brought us over here."

He dropped his glance to Skull Canyon again. The posse, as he judged it to be, had pulled up in confusion just south of the bulge. They were staring up the slope and Slade knew they could see him if he rode out of the shadow.

"Horse, we'll amble down and meet those gents," he said. "I'll bet you the one riding in front is hiding behind a tin plate." Shadow snorted and didn't accept the wager. Slade sent him pacing forward, plucked off his hat and waved it up and down. The posse-men waved reply and moved ahead, slowly. Shadow, snorting his disgust, went skittering down the steep slope.

As he neared the rimrock Slade saw that a hundred yards or so above where the drygulchers had been holed up it could be negotiated to the canyon floor. He urged Shadow down the shaley sag and a few minutes later he was riding down the canyon toward the posse, which had pulled up again and sat watching his approach.

Slightly in advance of his companions was a fresh-faced young fellow who, just as he suspected, was "hiding behind a tin plate"; in other words, he had a large nickel badge pinned to his sagging vest. Slade nodded to him.

"Howdy, Sheriff?" he greeted.

"What in blazes was going on up there?" the young sheriff demanded. "What was all the shooting about?"

"Well," Slade smiled as he drew rein, "there was a bunch of gents holed up on the rimrock like they were waiting for somebody. From the way they acted when you fellows showed up down to the south, I got a notion it was you they were waiting for, and I also got the idea that they didn't intend to throw you any bouquets of roses when you came around the bulge below here. So, not knowing for sure what it was all about but feeling it didn't look just right, I cut a few limbs off over their heads from the sag a piece. They appeared to decide they were overdue someplace else and went away from here by way of the side canyon over to the right."

The sheriff swore wholeheartedly, evidently having no trouble understanding the situation.

"Did you down any of the hellions?" he asked eagerly.

Slade shook his head. "No," he replied, "as I said, I didn't know for sure what it was all about and didn't want to chance making a mistake. I figured that if I had the wrong slant on things it would be easier to explain a few twigs and leaves knocked off the bushes than patches of skin off some heads."

"Reckon that's reasonable," the sheriff admitted, adding, "but I sure wish you hadn't been so particular. That was a bunch of snake-blooded hellions you threw lead over, and you can bet on that. Think you could identify them if you saw them again?"

Slade shook his head. "At six hundred yards faces are just a whitish blur," he replied obliquely. "One of them appeared to be a rather husky gent, but I'm not prepared to go any farther than that."

The sheriff nodded. "By the way, did you see anything of a herd of cows going this way, going fast?" he asked.

"Yes," Slade answered. "That's what made me sort of suspicious of those fellows on the rimrock. Those cows went past mighty fast and the men shoving them along waved friendly like to the bunch on the rock."

6

The sheriff swore again. "Those cows were widelooped off the Circle K spread over to the east of here," he explained. "We're chasing the hellions. How long since they went past?"

"More than an hour and a half, I'd say," Slade replied.

The sheriff swore for a third time, with greater vehemence. He glanced at the upper rim of the sun vanishing behind the crest of the slope.

"Nearly two hours ahead of us," he growled. "And in less than an hour it'll be black dark in these holes. They've done it again! No chance to trail them in the dark, and by morning they'll be plumb in the clear."

He turned to Slade and stuck out his hand. "Feller," he said, "my name's Sloan, Rance Sloan. I'm sheriff of Yoakum county and these boys are my deputies and a couple of specials." He rattled off several names. Slade supplied his own and shook hands all around.

"Reckon it's up to us to say much obliged mighty earnest," the sheriff continued. "You sure saved us from getting punctured hides. Those Nueces country sidewinders will stop at nothing."

"Nueces country?" Slade remarked interrogatively.

"That's right," said Sheriff Sloan. "A bunch of 'em ambled up here about four months back and squatted in this section, up to the north and west, and hell has been bustin' loose ever since. Well, reckon we might as well be heading back to town. Nothing more we can do down here. Maybe tomorrow we can try and pick up the trail, though there ain't much chance of trailing them through those cracks at any time, especially as they seem to know every hole and gulch and all the ways through to the west. Plenty of markets for slick-iron cows over the other side of the New Mexico line."

Slade nodded. "But before you head back to town, I'd like to have you ride up the sag to where that bunch was holed up," he said.

"Why?" asked the sheriff.

Again Slade's answer was oblique. "Did you see anybody around here besides myself?" he asked. The sheriff shook his head, his face puzzled.

"All you heard was some shooting and the story I told you, isn't that right?" Slade persisted.

"Reckon it is," the sheriff agreed, looking still more puzzled.

"Well," Slade continued, "isn't it just possible that later on you might get to thinking about what you saw and heard and didn't see? And isn't it also possible that you all of a sudden might recall that I held you up for quite a while, sufficient to allow those wideloopers to get a better start, and until it was very nearly dark?"

The sheriff shot him an admiring glance. "By gosh, you're right," he conceded. "I might have got to thinking just that. Feller, you're smart! All right, I'll ride up with you and look things over."

On the rimrock Slade pointed out the indubitable signs that several men and horses had occupied the spot only a short time before. The sheriff nodded his head and glanced down into the side canyon.

"And they dived into that crack, eh," he remarked. "I'm pretty sure they can reach the rangeland over to the west by way of it."

"I think you're right," Slade agreed. "I'm pretty sure I passed its mouth as I rode up from the south. It trends south pretty sharply and the trail across the hills doesn't follow it."

The sheriff nodded. "And once out there they could head any direction," he said. "Well, let's ride back down and head for town. Will be way past dark when we get there and I'm hungry as the devil already."

They had covered perhaps five miles and the canyon was growing shadowy when the sheriff suddenly jerked up his head. "Horses coming," he said. "Get set, boys, we're taking no chances. Sounds like quite a few of them."

"Three," Slade said.

The sheriff gave him a quick look and then turned his attention back to the trail ahead. A moment later three riders bulged from a straggle of growth.

"Danged if there ain't only three!" muttered the sheriff. "What kind of ears have you got anyhow? Hold it, boys, it's Just Bob Biggers and a couple of his hands. "Hi-yuh, Bigger?" he called. "What you fellers doing over here?"

The man addressed, a powerfully built individual with a square, muscle-packed, bad-tempered face and alert eyes returned the sheriff's greeting.

"We heard what had happened," he explained. "Figured maybe we'd better amble over and give you a hand if you happened to need it."

"A good notion," growled the sheriff, adding, "and if it hadn't been for this gent here, I reckon you'd have had the chore of packin' what was left of us back to town."

In terse sentences liberally sprinkled with lurid profanity he regaled the newcomer with an account of the recent happenings.

"So shake hands with Walt Slade, Bob," he concluded. "He sure came in mighty handy."

Biggers shook hands with a powerful grip. His companions, lean, efficient-looking men in rangeland garb also acknowledged the introduction.

"Bob owns the Double B spread right over to the east," the sheriff volunteered for Slade's benefit.

Slade nodded, his keen eyes taking in the three men and their riding gear. Only a person well acquainted with El Halcon's uncanny ability to absorb the smallest details in a single, all-embracing glance might possibly have detected his interest in that riding gear and particularly the well-scuffed boots of the riders. Those boots showed signs of having been in water no great time before.

CHAPTER TWO

BIGGERS AND HIS MEN reined around and both groups continued to the mouth of the canyon and turned sharply east through the deepening twilight. Half an hour or so of riding and Slade saw cattle grazing on the rich grass. There was still light enough for him to note that the majority of the cows bore Biggers' Double B brand, although quite a few were burned with a Circle K.

The posse veered slightly north and shortly afterward struck a travelled trail. Two more hours of riding and through the darkness the lights of a town became visible.

"That's Lucas, the county seat," Sheriff Sloan remarked to Slade. "She's quite a pueblo; a gathering place for riders from all over the section. And for quite a few hellions we could very well do without," he added in a grumbling voice. "They come from New Mexico and Oklahoma and other places. All 'pear to have to stop off here, like they used to do in old Tascosa years ago."

Upon reaching the town, which proved to be a considerable sprawl of buildings on the level prairie, the posse quickly dispersed in quest of food or other refreshment. Sheriff Sloan headed for his office to learn if any reports had come in during his absence. Slade was left with the Double B owner, Bob Biggers.

"Reckon you're in line for a bite to eat, eh?" remarked the rancher. "Figure the First Chance right down the street is your best bet."

"First I'd like to put up my horse," Slade said.

"A good stable right down this next alley," said Biggers. "I'll herd you to it. Old Lafe's got a room or two for rent up over the stalls, too, if you like to sleep close to your horse."

They turned into the alley and quickly reached the livery stable. A large tree grew close to the door and a lantern hung on a pole at the street corner dappled the front of the building with shadows cast by the spreading limbs.

Repeated hammering on the door finally aroused the stable keeper who appeared in boots and a long nightshirt as white as his hair and beard.

"Brought you some business, Lafe," Biggers announced. "This feller is okay."

"Sure he's okay," creaked Lafe. "Couldn't handle a horse like that if he wasn't."

Biggers chuckled. "He's some horse, all right," he agreed. "Never saw a finer. Well, Slade, I got some chores to do. Expect I'll see you later in the First Chance if you stick around there a spell."

After Shadow's wants were taken care of, old Lafe led the way up the stairs to a clean little room in the front of the building, the door of which opened outward at the stairhead.

"You can leave your rig in here," he told Slade. "Everything will be plumb safe; nobody sleeping here tonight but me, and I'm dang particular as to who sleeps here any time. I'll light the lamp and then I'm going back to bed; was up most of last night with a sick horse."

The room was small, furnished with a bed and a couple of chairs. A window opened in the far wall, through which the leaves and branches of the tree were revealed by the lamplight.

"Ain't much to look at but it's clean and no bugs," said Lafe. "Reckon you've slept in worse places."

"I have," Slade admitted. "This looks okay."

Old Lafe pottered across to the window which stood wide open. He removed the supporting stick and lowered the sash.

"Looks a mite like rain," he explained. "Besides, it's sort of cool tonight. If you want more air when you go to bed you can raise it again; the stick's right here on the ledge. You going out to eat? Okay, here's a key to the front door. I always keep it locked at night. Just amble in and go to bed whenever you're ready. If you should happen to need me I sleep in the room at the end of the hall. The one between is empty tonight."

Slade thanked the keeper and departed in search of something to eat. He had no difficulty locating the First Chance, a big saloon with ample accommodations for hungry patrons. He sat down at a table and ordered a meal. While he was eating, Sheriff Rance Sloan entered. He spotted Slade, nodded to him and approached the bar. After downing a drink he crossed to Slade's table and sat down.

"Think I'll have something myself if you don't mind," he said. "Nope, nothing else has busted loose, but I ain't hopeful. Not so long as them dang Nueces hellions are swaller-forking all over the lot.

"I thought I was getting a break today," he continued, picking petulantly at his knife and fork. "This is the first time the devils ever pulled a raid in daylight; before they've always worked at night. Val Russell of the Circle K had got a herd together on his south pasture, a bunch of prime cows he figured to run over into Oklahoma and sell to a feller there who wanted them for breeding purposes. I got a notion the hellions might make a try for that herd—they always seem to know everything that's going on in the section—so me and the boys were ambling down there to hole up tonight against the chance they would make a try for it."

The sheriff paused to roll and light a cigarette. As he touched a match to the tip, a man entered and passed close to the table; a heavily built, well proportioned man of medium height and age with a bronzed face and dark hair. He nodded to the sheriff and Sloan nodded back, a bit shortly, Slade thought, which was verified by the sheriff's next remark.

"That's Carter Renshaw who owns the Bradded R up to the north," he said. "All right, I reckon, but seems a bit too friendly with those Neuces hellions to suit me. Where was I? Oh, yes, I was telling you how me and the boys were riding down to the Circle K.

"Well, all of a sudden here comes Billy Taylor, one of the Circle K hands, skalleyhooting for fair. He had a bullet hole through his shoulder and was in purty bad shape. Taylor'd been handed the chore of keeping that herd together today and the hellions jumped him in broad daylight, gunned him and run off the herd. He was hard hit but managed to get in the clear and he was forking a mighty fast horse. He pulled away from them and headed for town and met us on the way. I figured the devils would shove the herd into the west hills by way of Skull Canyon and I was right. Figured I had a good chance to catch up with them before dark. Sent one of the boys to town with Taylor and the rest of us headed for Skull Canyon. I think we might have caught up with them if it hadn't been for that shindig in the canyon that delayed us.

"Not that I'm complaining about being delayed," he added hastily. "Otherwise I reckon we might be out there right now, waiting for the buzzards."

"Did Taylor get a look at the men who shot him?" Slade asked.

The sheriff shook his head. "Nope, he said they had handkerchiefs tied over their faces, and I reckon he wasn't in very good shape to see anything. Not much doubt in my mind as to who's responsible, though; them Nueces sidewinders or some of their friends, you can lay to that. There'll never be any peace in this section so long as they're operating here."

"You say they settled over to the west of here?" Slade remarked.

"Yes, to the west and north, beyond where Skull Canyon opens out of the hills," Sloan replied. "Good range over there. Nobody used it till they showed up although now and then some strays from the spreads to the east and north of here got over that far. A pity some of the boys didn't file on it and get title. Then they could have rooted those horned toads out before they dug in proper."

"Did the Nueces men get title?" Slade asked.

"Reckon they did," Sloan admitted.

"And they aren't friendly toward the owners over here. Why?"

The sheriff swore disgustedly. "I'm danged if I know, or anybody else over here for that matter," he said. "But ain't friendly' is putting it plumb mild. They don't want to have nothing to do with nobody. Scairt somebody will catch on to their slick iron tricks, I reckon. Anybody who tries to amble over there gets warned off, sometimes with lead whistling around his ears. They're sure an unsociable bunch, all right, whatever the reason. Seem to be plumb on the prod against everybody."

"Funny," Slade observed, "I've been down in the Nueces country and always found folks there easy to get along with."

"Reckon this nest of sidewinders got run out of there," Sloan grunted. "Don't see how any decent community could put up with them for long. Some of the boys hereabouts are for riding over and sending them back where they came from with burrs under their tails; but naturally as a law officer I couldn't stand for that, and Bob Biggers and Carter Renshaw both pointed out that it would play right into their hands."

"They've got something there," Slade agreed.

"Biggers and Renshaw ain't got overly much use for each other. Biggers figures, too, that Renshaw is a bit too friendly with the Nueces bunch but they agree on that point, saying such a row wouldn't be worth what the cost is liable to be," the sheriff continued.

"Decidedly so," Slade nodded.

"But there's a limit," the sheriff declared. "They'll go too far sometime if they keep on and then there'll be real trouble."

"Yes, another Pleasant Valley war," Slade commented grimly. "I've a notion Texas can do without that. The Horrel-Higgins row was bad enough, but I gather it would be small potatoes to what could happen here."

"Reckon it would," Sloan nodded. "There's about a hundred of those hellions over there, and maybe three times that scattered around this section over here. Would be quite a shindig while it lasted."

"And everybody the loser," Slade said. "You say the man who passed here a few minutes ago, Renshaw, I believe you said his name is—he's standing at the far end of the bar—you say he's on friendly terms with the Nueces people?"

"Oh, maybe that's putting it a bit too strong," Sloan admitted, "but he says he's talked with some of the younger hands when they were riding past his place on their way to Plaino up to the northeast, where they do their buying, and 'lows they don't seem such bad sorts. Hell! Maybe he's right about the younger fellows. It's the owners who keep stirring the hell kettle, I guess, with old Tom Wardell, who I understand is the big he-wolf of the pack, leading in the sod pawing."

"Tom Wardell," Slade repeated. "A sort of head man, eh?"

"That's right," said the sheriff. "I heard it said he was up here scouting around before any of the rest showed up. Just how they got here without being spotted nobody seems to know. Nobody saw 'em come. All of a sudden they were here, squattin' on the good rangeland up there. Sundown riders, I reckon, and that sort never is up to any good."

By adroit questioning, Slade learned, without the sheriff catching on that he desired to, that a trail led from town to the holdings of the Nueces men, a trail that passed by old Tom Wardell's ranchhouse.

"Here come Bob Biggers and his boys," the sheriff remarked. "He can hold more redeye than any other man in Yoakum County."

Biggers waved a greeting and grinned, showing crooked but very white teeth. He lumbered on to the far end of the bar, his two hands treading lithely at his heels, and bellowed for drinks.

Biggers had a rumbling voice and didn't bother to keep it down. It soon became apparent that he was regaling the crowd around him with an account of the happenings in Skull Canyon.

"And he forks just about the finest black cayuse you ever laid eyes on," Slade heard him say. "If I wasn't so scairt of old Lafe's horse pistol I'd be of a notion of trying to slip that critter out of the stable tonight. Ever see that horse pistol Lafe keeps in his room? You could shove a nail keg in the bore. If he ever cuts loose with it half this town will be blowed off the map."

Sheriff Sloan chuckled. "If you aim to coil your twine in this section I've a notion Biggers would take you on," he observed to Slade. "He 'pears to have taken a shine to you."

"Might be a good notion," Slade conceded. "Appears to be an interesting section."

"Too dang interesting of late," Sloan grumbled, "but you wouldn't have any trouble tieing onto a job if you aim to squat. Always in need of tophands hereabouts."

"Biggers an old-timer here?" Slade asked.

The sheriff shook his head. "Nope, been here less than a year," he replied. "We've been getting quite a few new folks of late. Reckon there's getting to be considerable crowding down around the Brazos and the Trinity. Carter Renshaw has only been here about six months, and the same goes for the Persinger brothers over to the east, and the Grahams, too. Lots of state land up here, or was, and folks are beginning to realize that the Panhandle is the coming cow country of Texas. Well, I think I'll turn in."

"Reckon I could stand a little ear pounding myself," Slade said. "Slept out last night and it was sort of cool."

"A mite too late in the year for comfortable chuck line riding," agreed the sheriff. "Better settle down till next spring."

"You may have a notion there," he conceded. "And it looks like a good section, all right, the grass appears excellent and the range easy to work. How about water? I didn't notice any streams while we were riding over Biggers' holdings."

"Oh, we've got enough to keep going," Sloan replied. "There aren't any creeks on Biggers' land, only waterholes fed by springs, but they're good ones and they run little trickles deep enough to wet a cow's nose."

Slade nodded again. He was thinking of Bob Biggers' wet boots, and visualizing the five drygulchers storming across the canyon creek through water stirrup-deep.

CHAPTER THREE

"WELL, SO LONG," SAID SLOAN. "May see you tomorrow if you're sticking around, that is if I ain't skalleyhootin' off somewhere chasin' my tail as I've been doing of late. And much obliged again for what you did this afternoon. I won't forget it." With a wave of his hand he left the saloon.

Slade watched him go and his eyes mirrored approval. A nice young fellow trying hard to do his duty. A bit young and inexperienced for the job, perhaps; an old-timer would never have gone barging into that canyon like he did today. It was a perfect set-up for a drygulching and a peace officer with experience would know that people who steal cows don't miss any bets. The sheriff should have been highly suspicious of a widelooping in broad daylight with the chance of pursuit being hot on the heels of the rustlers. He should have realized that there was a catch somewhere and should have been on the lookout accordingly. But he'd learn, if he managed to live long enough.

Slade had come to the Tucumcari Desert country on a definite mission, but it was beginning to look like he might get sidetracked from his original chore, but perhaps the two angles would tie up. He'd try and see about that later, making his first move the following morning.

Settling himself comfortably in his chair he lighted another cigarette and watched the crowd in the big room with interest. The First Chance patrons, so far as he could see, with the possible exception of Bob Biggers and Carter Renshaw, the Bradded R owner, both of whom appeared to possess a certain individuality, were an average cow country bunch with nothing outstanding about them. He suspected that Biggers was considerable of a character, while Renshaw had a self-sufficient look about him. Both able cattlemen, doubtless, their ability proven by the fact that they had not been content to remain hired hands and had acquired property of their own.

A little later Slade paid for his meal and departed from the First Chance. He walked slowly up the street to the alley upon which the livery stable fronted. It was dark in the narrow lane, the gloom relieved only by the feeble gleam of the pole-hung lantern at the corner.

In accordance with the habit of years Slade narrowly eyed his surroundings as he entered the alley, probing the deeper shadow beneath the tree, raising his glance to its tangle of branches that were swathed in blackness, scanning the front of the building.

Abruptly he slowed his pace, his eyes fixed on the building front. The window he distinctly remembered as being closed when he left the room now stood wide open. Slowing still more he gazed at the silent black square. He recalled that old Lafe had shut it, 'lowing that there might be rain and besides it was cool. It didn't seem reasonable that the stablekeeper would have returned to the room later and opened the window.

As he approached the stable door, slowly and watchfully, he wondered how close the tree branches above came to the window sill, close enough perhaps to make it possible to raise the sash from the outside. Which would mean that it was also possible to enter the room by way of the window. But why? A little job of burgling, or perhaps an attempt to steal a horse? Well, if that was tried on Shadow the whole town would know about it and would assemble to identify the remains of the widelooper, what was left to identify.

But there was another angle to consider. Somebody might be holed up in the room. Why, again? That was a question El Halcon preferred to have the answer to before entering the room. His eyes never left the black rectangle as he approached the stable door, but he could detect nothing breaking the even darkness of the opening; and if somebody was inside the room, unless he leaned out the window he could hardly note the approach of anybody walking softly in the shadow as he, Slade, had done.

With the greatest care he thrust the key into the lock. The well oiled mechanism turned silently and the door swung open without a creak. Slade stepped inside and closed it just as softly.

The inside of the stable was dusky, the gloom relieved only by a faint glow seeping down the stairs from a bracket lamp in the hall above. It was silent save for one thing, something that gave Slade concern and quickened all his senses to hair-trigger alertness. Shadow was blowing softly and persistently through his nose, a sure sign that a stranger was somewhere near, and it seemed to Slade that he rolled his eyes upward, although doubtless that was but a figment of overwrought imagination.

Just the same The Hawk was in no mood to take chances. At the foot of the stairs he paused to slip off his boots. Carrying them in one hand, the other close to his gun butt, he ascended the stairs in utter silence, testing each tread before resting his full weight upon it. The staircase was firmly constructed and gave out no tell-tale creaks. He turned into the narrow hall that separated the rooms from the haymow and paused beside the door of his room.

For long moments he stood listening intently and heard nothing. The silence was as of a tomb. But just the same he hesitated at opening the door. He would be outlined against the lighted hall if he did so. For another moment he waited and listened. Then he placed the boots on the floor and drew his left-hand gun. Snugging against the wall he reached out with his right hand and slowly and carefully turned the knob. When he was sure the bolt was all the way back, he flipped the door open. It swung wide. Through the opening glinted a ray of reflected light, and that was all. Still no sound broke the utter silence, but the subtle sixth sense that develops in men who ride alone with danger as a stirrup companion had abruptly set up a noiseless clamor in his brain, and Slade had learned not to ignore the warnings of that silent but vigilant monitor. He remained flattened against the wall, wondering what the devil to do. To all appearances the room was empty, but...

Abruptly he got an idea. He picked up one of the boots, removed his hat and balanced it on top of it. Then he gripped the boot by the heel and crouched low, holding the boot and the poised hat above his head. He thrust it slowly around the edge of the jamb to simulate a man peering cautiously into the room.

There was a crashing report, the boot was knocked from his hand and slammed against the far wall. Another shot boomed and a bullet thudded into the wall. Slade whipped out his right-hand gun and sprayed the room with slugs, hugging the wall, shifting his hand back and forth. Thumb hooked over the cocked hammer, he held his fire and listened intently. His ears were ringing from the bellow of the reports but he thought he heard a thrashing, rustling sound followed by a solid thump. He hesitated an instant, then realized that the sounds had come from outside the room. He slipped through the door, sidled along the inner wall and eyed the open window. Nothing was to be seen but the tangle of tree branches beyond. Slade glided to the window and peered out. It was too dark to make out details but he could see the shadowy shape of a large limb just beyond and a few feet below the window ledge. The growth was so thick that he could not get a glimpse of the ground below.

"Well, that's that!" he exclaimed aloud as he slipped back to retrieve his hat and boots.

Down the hall a door banged open. Old Lafe rushed out brandishing a cocked horse pistol about a yard long. Slade hurriedly ducked out of line.

"Put that danged cannon down!" he shouted. "If it goes off there won't be any roof left. Lower the hammer!"

"What the devil's going on here?" bellowed Lafe as he obeyed instructions.

"A little try at burgling, I'd say," Slade told him. "Some jigger threw lead at me when I opened the door and ducked to the ground by way of that tree out there. I don't think he got anything—there are my rifle and saddle and pouches where I left them."

"More likely he was after your horse," Lafe growled, sniffing suspiciously, like an animal that scents danger. "How'd he get in?"

"The window was open, and I remember you closed it before we went out," Slade replied.

Lafe stumped across the room, his nightshirt flapping about his bare legs, and peered out the window.

"Come in by way of those tree limbs," he growled. "Wouldn't have had much trouble prying the window open from the outside. Uh-huh, I'll bet he figured to sneak downstairs and lift one of the horses, yours, most likely. That big black must attract considerable attention."

"If he'd tried to put a hand on Shadow he sure would have needed a window to jump out, what was left of him," Slade observed grimly.

"Wouldn't be a bit surprised," agreed Lafe. "That cayuse looked me over mighty close when I came up to him last evening, and I get along with horses."

"I noticed that," Slade replied. "I decided it wasn't necessary to introduce you two before you stalled him."

Old Lafe chuckled creakily. "Sounds funny, to be introduced to a horse," he said, "but just the same it makes sense. Well, I'm going back to bed, but first maybe we'd better hang a blanket over that darn window."

"Oh, I don't think the hellion will come back for another try, not tonight, anyhow," Slade replied.

"Okay," grunted Lafe. "Look at the bullet holes in the wall! Mighty lucky you weren't in line when he cut loose. They're up mighty high, though. Reckon they would have gone over your head."

Slade didn't argue the point, but he knew the slugs had not gone high, not when they passed through the open door. The hole through one of his boots amply attested to the fact. The fellow had been standing on the big branch below the window and his gun barrel had been slanted up a bit, that was all.

"I sort of stepped aside when I opened the door," he remarked casually, being content to let the stablekeeper make his own interpretation of the incident.

Old Lafe nodded and went back to his room. Slade closed the door, sat down on the bed and lighted a cigarette. It had been a nice try, all right, and if he hadn't noticed the open window it would have worked. Nervy and patient devil! Had waited until what he considered just the right moment, even though he must have begun to suspect that his intended victim realized something wasn't just as it should be. The question was, who was responsible? Bob Biggers had showed him to the stable and of course would have been able to guess where he would sleep, but Biggers had been sounding off in the saloon and any of his hearers could have deduced the same thing.

Slade had no real reason for suspecting Biggers aside from the coincidence of Biggers and his men having wet boots right after the five drygulchers had assuredly gotten theirs wet in the canyon creek. The sheriff said there were no deep streams running across Biggers' land, only waterholes. Of course he and his men might have been digging out a silted waterhole and had gotten their boots wet in the course of the operation. That had to be considered. But if the attempt on his life had been in retaliation for the part he played in frustrating the drygulching of the sheriff's posse it hinted at a close-knit and alert organization that wasted no time evening up a score.

Which brought Slade around to wondering if there could be a possible connection between the attempt and what had brought him into the section in the first place. He thought over his interview with Captain Jim McNelty a couple of weeks previous.

"Walt," Captain Jim had said, "I got a tip that Ellis Dawson has showed up in Texas again and is operating in the Tucumcari Desert country up in the Panhandle."

"The devil he is!" Slade exclaimed.

"That's right," said Captain Jim. "I got the first tip a couple of months ago while you were on that chore down around Galveston and didn't pay it much mind, but reports have kept coming in. Folks who should know what they are talking about swear it's Dawson, all right. Let's see, you just about wiped out his bunch over around Doan's Crossing, didn't you?"

"Yes," Slade admitted, "but I didn't wipe out Dawson. I wasn't riding Shadow that day and he was forking a mighty good horse. He pulled away from me and gave me the slip and I could never pick up his trail. I figured he got over the Oklahoma line into the hills there."

"Which makes him sort of unfinished business for you, eh?"

"That's right," Slade replied grimly.

"You never got a very good look at him?"

"Never did," Slade agreed. "About all I can say of him is that he is a medium-sized gent, but built husky and wears heavy black whiskers. Not that the whiskers mean much; whiskers can be shaved and grown again."

"Everybody seems sort of hazy as to what he looks like," resumed Captain Jim, "but they're pretty well agreed on the way he operates. He's a tough hombre."

"Yes, he's that," Slade nodded. "Specializes in widelooping cows with stage and bank and train robberies thrown in for good measure. He's got plenty of notches on his guns, although I don't figure he's the sort that files notches; takes killings a little too casually to keep tally, I'd say. Notorious for drygulchings, has wiped out whole outfits. Yes, he's bad, a quick-draw man and a crack shot, but something more important: he thinks as fast as he draws and plans things down to the minutest detail and pulls them off like clockwork. A lot more dangerous, in consequence, than the average brush popping owlhoot who makes mistakes."

Captain Jim nodded and drummed on his desk. "Think he'd recognized you if he saw you again?" he asked.

"Not beyond the realm of possibility," Slade admitted. "Not that it makes any particular difference."

"I'd say it makes considerable, especially when you're not sure you'd recognize him," Captain Jim commented dryly, "but as you say, he's sort of unfinished business for you."

"So I guess I'd better take a little ride up to the Panhandle," Slade smiled.

"Well, if you feel that way I reckon there's not much sense in me trying to stop you," Captain Jim chuckled, knowing perfectly well that his lieutenant and ace-man was itching for another go at the outlaw who eluded him a couple of years before.

"We're going to miss that big feller when he takes a notion to leave the Rangers," Captain Jim remarked to his clerk after Slade had taken his departure.

"Think he'll really pull out some time?" the clerk asked.

"Oh, sure, very likely he will, sooner or later," the captain replied. "Walt's a college man, you know. He studied engineering and had figured to take a specialized post-graduate course, but shortly after he finished college, blizzards and droughts and widelooping caused his dad's ranch to fail up. Right after that the old man died and Walt was sort of at loose ends. He'd worked with me some during summer vacations and I reckon Ranger work sort of got under his skin. Anyhow when I suggested he tie up with the Rangers for a while he did. He's always studying in his spare time and I reckon he's pretty near got what he figured to get out of the post-grad. But there's no doubt but the Rangers have got hold of him and he'll stay with us for a while yet. Has made considerable of a reputation during the years he's been with the corps."

" 'The top Ranger of them all,' " the clerk quoted.

"Yep, that's what they call him," Captain Jim agreed. "He's a good deal of a legend throughout the Southwest now. Got a funny mixed reputation. He has a habit of working under cover and quite a few times he's cleaned up a chore, largely with his guns, without revealing his Ranger connections. Quite a few folks, including some sheriffs, will tell you that if El Halcon isn't an owlhoot he misses being one by the skin of his teeth, and tooth skin is mighty thin. Walt says it helps in his work and never takes the trouble to deny it."

"The Mexicans named him El Halcon, I believe," remarked the clerk.

"That's right," nodded the commander. "They all swear by him and think he's the finest thing that ever walked with the forked end down. El Halcon means The Hawk. He sort of reminds you of one of those big gray-eyed mountain fellers that will give an eagle his come-uppance, in appearances and the way he moves. He's quite a jigger, all right."

"Well, he's out after a mighty bad hombre this time," Captain Jim concluded. "Hope Dawson won't know him when they meet. Would give the hellion an advantage."

CHAPTER FOUR

SLADE HAD AN EARLY BREAKFAST at the First Chance. Then he saddled up and rode out of town, headed north. Without difficulty he found the trail Sheriff Sloan mentioned the evening before and continued on his way with the rising sun slanting steadily toward his back as the trail veered westward.

"A pretty country," he told Shadow, "a mighty pretty country. Enough and more here for everybody if everybody would just work together and take what it has to give. Nothing for anybody to complain about here, except the trouble they bring on themselves."

Some twelve miles northwest of town the trail wound over low, brush covered hills that had replaced the level range. To the right was thick chaparral crowding the track, to the left a long wooded slope that rolled up to the distant skyline.

Slade redoubled his caution and rode watchful and alert, probing thickets and clump of chimney rock with a gaze that missed nothing. But for all his care the first indication of a hidden gunman was the crackling, splitting passage of a high-power rifle bullet a few inches above his head. The first slug was instantly followed by a second that fanned his face with its lethal breath. He sent Shadow sideways into the sheltering growth, dismounted and glared wrathfully up the opposite slope.

The heat-shimmered haze obscured his view and hid any tell-tale wisping of smoke, but very quickly he spotted a blue-jay wheeling and darting angrily above a thicket about four hundred yards up the sag.

For several minutes Slade intently watched the bird. He nodded with satisfaction. He was convinced that in that particular thicket was where the hellion was holed up, and thanks to his feathered friend up there, the devil was very likely to be in for a surprise.

"You just take it easy for a spell, and no singing," he told Shadow. "That jigger will figure he's got us both hunting cover over here and will have his eyes in this direction. Now for a bit of scout work."

Making sure his guns were free in their holsters, he made his way through the growth, slid across the trail a couple of hundred yards farther west and entered the brush at the foot of the slope. With the greatest care he worked up the sag, veering to the left. Finally he decided he was above the spot where the drygulcher was holed up. The jay had settled into the brush once more and there was nothing to mark the particular thicket that sheltered the rifleman. And then, while he was debating a course of action, Shadow unwittingly did him a favor.

The horse had doubtless grown weary of standing in one place and had moved a little, perhaps in search of forage. In so doing he agitated the chaparral, causing the tops to sway. Instantly the drygulcher cut loose at the movement. The rifle clanged. Up shot the jay, swearing profusely. A thin grin stretched Slade's lips. He glided forward through the brush and a little to one side. With snail-like progress he approached the thicket where the bird had been feeding or had its nest. Worming his way between the trunks he covered a few more yards, raised his head and peered downward.

Under a thick bristle of mesquite ran an irregular ledge and back of this ledge, just a few yards below where The Hawk crouched, was a clump of solider shadow.

As Slade watched, the shadow moved slightly and coughed. He slid forward again and was almost within arm's reach of the man behind the ledge when the dry stick beneath the leaves snapped under his weight.

The man whirled about, Slade caught the gleam of the upward flung rifle barrel. His fist shot out with all his two hundred pounds of bone and muscle behind it. There was a crunching thud, the roar of the rifle flinging a bullet to the sky. Then the drygulcher collapsed in a motionless huddle. Slade bent over him, first poised to strike a second time, but the fellow was completely out.

El Halcon eased back on his heels and regarded the motionless form a moment. Then he turned the man over on his back to reveal his face.

"Tarnations! just a kid!" he muttered. "Hope I didn't bust his jaw. Hmmm this may work out pretty good. Reckon a little act for this gent's benefit is in order."

He carefully examined the already swelling jaw where his fist had landed. Under the probing of his fingers the unconscious man groaned. Slade sat back on his heels again to await developments.

The drygulcher was a rather nice-looking young fellow clad in rangeland garb. He could not be, Slade decided, much over twenty, but plenty old enough to fang. Slade plucked a sixgun from the other's holster and thrust it under his own belt. He picked up the boy's rifle, an excellent weapon, and cast it into the bushes.

A few minutes later the young cowboy rolled his head, groaned again and opened wide blue eyes. He raised himself on his elbows and stared dazedly at the grim figure squatting opposite him and suggestively fingering the lock of a long-barrelled Colt. His vision cleared and an expression of fright spread over his face. Slade's voice, grinding at him like steel on ice, didn't help matters.

"What's the big notion, throwing lead at folks on an open trail?" The Hawk demanded. "Fellow, you're mighty lucky you only got a bust on the jaw. I should have gut-shot you through the back and left you to die sweating. That's still not a bad notion."

The cowboy cringed back from El Halcón's terrible eyes. "I—I—I didn't try to hit you," he yammered. "I just aimed to scare you and turn you back. I was just obeying orders."

"Whose orders?" Slade demanded.

"Old Tom's, my dad's, old Tom Wardell. I'm young Tom."

"Uh-huh, and you got a mighty good chance never to be 'old' Tom," Slade remarked grimly, still fingering his Colt. "Why did you throw lead at me?"

"B-because we don't allow nobody to ride up to our *casa*— nobody from over east," young Tom sputtered.

"What you scared of?" Slade asked.

"We ain't scairt," denied young Tom. "But after what happened to Dad and the boys the first time they come up in this section we don't take no chances."

Slade considered this statement, the concentration furrow deepening between his black brows, but he did not ask further enlightenment at the moment.

"Don't allow anybody to ride up to your *casa*, eh?" he observed. "Well, I've a notion that rule is going to get broken. Where's your horse?"

"Over in the brush," said young Tom, gesturing to the right.

Slade stood up, twirling the cocked Colt around his finger by the trigger guard.

"Get him," he ordered, "and don't forget, I'm right behind you, and I haven't decided yet just what I'm going to do with you."

Young Tom shivered. He scrambled to his feet, swaying a little and tenderly fingering his swollen jaw. He led the way to where his horse, a good-looking bay, was tethered.

"All right," Slade directed, "down the slope to the trail."

Young Wardell obeyed without demur. When they reached the trail, Slade whistled to Shadow. The black horse came crashing out of the brush, ears pricked forward inquiringly.

For the moment Tom Wardell forgot his unpleasant predicament. "Golly, what a horse!" he exclaimed. "Gosh! supposed I'd held a mite low and plugged him! Never would have forgiven myself."

Slade suppressed a grin. Wardell's concern for the horse had its humorous side, under the circumstances. The glance he bent on the cowboy's back was anything but unfriendly, but when Wardell turned around he was confronted by a bleak face and hard eyes. He mounted in obedience to Slade's gesture with the Colt. Slade also swung into the saddle.

"All right," he said, "head for your *casa* I want to talk to your dad."

Wardell stared at him unbelievingly. "Feller," he exclaimed, "you can't get away with that. We got men up there who can dot a lizard's eye with a sixgun at thirty paces. They'll drill you out of the saddle before you have time to talk."

"Maybe," Slade conceded, "but you sure won't enjoy it." He fished a bit of twine from his pocket as he spoke. Next he drew the trigger of his gun all the way back and lashed it securely against the guard. Then he cocked the gun.

"See how it works?" he said. "She's at full cock and with the trigger tied back only the weight of my thumb keeps the hammer from dropping and busting the cartridge. The muzzle is going to be right against your back and if anything happens to me, well, I reckon my thumb would slip off the hammer."

Young Tom saw without difficulty. His face turned a bit green, his eyes widened with terror.

"G-good gosh, feller!" he stuttered, "I can't guarantee some-body won't throw lead at you when they see you, per-tickler if they see you holding that gun on me."

"Well," Slade replied cheerfully, "reckon that's your look-out. Figure you better try sort of hard to get me through, don't you?"

Wardell made a moaning sound and began to sweat. But in obedience to Slade's pre-emptory order he started his horse up the trail.

As they progressed, young Tom's nervousness increased. "Say, feller," he gulped, "suppose the boys don't catch on quick enough and an accident happens?"

"Don't let it bother you," Slade returned pleasantly. "I'm holding the muzzle a bit low and I reckon you'll live long enough after the slug goes through to explain things to them."

Young Tom made a noise like a pig with a rattlesnake's tail stuck in its throat and was apparently reduced to a quivering jelly.

They had covered perhaps two miles when the brush fell away and Slade saw a comfortable-looking ranchhouse set in a grove of wide-spread cottonwoods. A number of men were busy about the yard. They looked up at the sound of hoofs and stared, hands dropping to their guns.

"What the devil?" Slade heard somebody say. Then a moment later, "Hey! that big feller's holding a gun on Tom!"

There was a clutching of weapons. Young Tom let out a yowl of anguish.

"Hold it!" he squalled. "Don't move, nobody! Don't come close! Stay right where you are! The trigger of that dang thing's tied back and if you drop him I'll get it, too, right through the back! I'm taking him to see Dad!"

"Looks more like he's taking you to see Dad," somebody remarked.

While the hands stared in slack-jawed amazement Slade sent his shivering charge straight for the ranchhouse door. Aroused by the tumult, two men stepped out onto the porch. One was a big old man whose frosty blue eyes were very much like young Tom's. Slade rightly guessed he was Tom Wardell, senior. His companion was small and wizened, his face a network of wrinkles, but his little black eyes were wonderfully bright and youthful.

"Hold it, Dad!" young Tom howled before his father could get out a word. "Hold it, Dobie! Don't move! This hellion has got me hogtied!"

They reined in at the veranda. Slade motioned his captive to dismount. He unforked at the same instant, the gun still hard against young Tom's back. In single file they mounted the steps to confront the astounded pair on the veranda. Old Tom seemed about ready to suffer an apoplectic stroke. Dobie, the range boss, appeared suddenly vastly amused by something.

Slade carefully lowered the hammer of his gun and flashed the Colt into its sheath with a move too swift for the eye to follow. Then he sat down, uninvited, in a homemade chair with a rawhide bottom that creaked under his weight.

With a hollow moan of relief, young Tom sagged against a post and wiped the sweat from his face. Old Tom glared at the imperturbable Hawk who had fished out the makin's and was rolling a cigarette with the slim fingers of his left hand.

"Say!" old Tom burst out, "what the devil is to keep us from plugging you right now?"

"Nothing, I reckon," Slade replied, his gray eyes dancing, "only—you won't."

"How you know we won't?" roared old Tom, his mustache bristling in his scarlet face.

"Well?" Slade asked, "Will you?"

Old Tom gulped, sputtered, glared. He spun on his heel and waved to the stupefied cowhands in the yard.

"Come up here, boys!" he bawled. "Come and look over a gent full of loco weed to his ears! Come on, he's worth looking at!"

The punchers moved forward to the foot of the steps and regarded Slade solemnly. His laughing gray eyes met their concerted stare and suddenly he smiled, the flashing white smile of El Halcon, that women, and men, found irresistible.

" 'Pears to me to have all his marbles," an old rannie remarked. The others nodded sober agreement.

"Everybody's loco!" bellowed old Tom. He glared at Slade, his glance dropped to the Ranger's heavy Colts slung low against his thighs, the butts flaring out from his sinewy hips, and an idea seemed to strike him.

"Two-gun, quick-draw man, eh?" he rumbled. "Say, did those hellions over to the east bring you in here to do their gun-slinging for them?"

"Nope," Slade replied.

Old Tom still looked suspicious. "How the devil do I know they didn't?" he demanded.

"Because I just told you so," Slade smiled.

Old Tom fairly danced with anger. "Then what in blazes do you want here?" he asked.

"Well, seeing as you ask me," Slade replied, "a bite to eat wouldn't go bad—I'm hungry."

Old Tom threw out his hands in a despairing gesture. "Come on in," he said, "while I go tell the cook to pizen you. Pete," he bellowed, "take that black horse to the barn and give him fodder."

Slade rose to his feet, nodded okay to Shadow, and followed Dobie into the living room. The little range boss seemed filled to bursting with some delicious secret all his own. His eyes snapped and sparkled as he lead the way into the house.

"Come along," Wardell called over his shoulder. "Soap and towels in back if you want to wash up first. Maybe nobody will shoot you, but I ain't promising."

An old Mexican cook was busy in the kitchen as Slade passed through. He started, eyes wide.

"*Capitan!*" he murmured and bowed his head as to a shrine. Slade's own head moved sideways in barely perceptible gesture.

Keen-eyed old Tom Wardell heard and saw, but he said nothing.

Slade didn't get shot while he washed up. He returned to the living-room, smiling at the old cook as he passed through the kitchen, and sat down. Old Tom lumbered to the foot of the stairs and let out a bellow.

"Dolores!" he shouted. "Come on down here, we're going to eat, and I want you to see a young whippersnapper plumb off his mental reservation."

"Coming, Dad," answered a sweet low voice. A moment later a girl tripped down the stairs. She wasn't very big, but her figure, Slade thought, was well nigh perfect. She had flame-colored hair, sweetly turned red lips and eyes much like young Tom's only wider and of a deeper blue.

Slade rose to his feet, towering over all present. Old Tom shot him a look.

"I didn't catch the particular name you're using right now," he said meaningly. Slade supplied it, his eyes dancing.

"Dolores, you heard what he calls himself," said old Tom. "Slade, this is my daughter Dolores. I figure she ain't quite as feather-brained as her brother but that ain't saying much."

"Dad is always like this when he's hungry," the girl said, extending a little sun-golden hand. Slade bowed over it with courtly grace. Old Tom grumbled under his mustache, young Tom fingered his sore jaw and grinned, and winced. Dobie chuckled.

Slade enjoyed an excellent meal. He sat between Dolores and young Tom and conversed easily with both. Old Tom ate largely in silence, but his temper appeared to improve with food. Later they retired to the living room and lighted cigarettes. Slade smoked for a few minutes and abruptly asked old Tom a question.

"Mr. Wardell," he said. "I gather that you and your neighbors over to the east aren't getting along together any too well?"

Old Tom snorted. "Who in blazes could get along with a bunch of sidewinders who pulled what they did on me the first time I was up this way?" he countered.

Slade considered a moment. "Suppose you tell me just what happened?" he suggested.

Wardell hesitated, fingering his mustache. It was Sime Dobie who spoke up.

"Tom," he said, "I believe it would be a good notion to tell this feller all about it, and listen to what he has to say. I've a notion he sort of has a way with folks."

Young Tom nodded emphatically, and caressed his swollen jaw. Dolores did not speak, but her big eyes said plenty.

Wardell still hesitated, but there was something about the steady gaze of the tall man in the chair opposite him that invited, or rather compelled, confidence. Before he knew it, he was recounting his tragic first experience with the section.

Tom Wardell was not an educated man but he was a good story teller, with an excellent memory for details, and Walt Slade quickly began to get an accurate and composite picture of what happened.

CHAPTER FIVE

O LD TOM WARDELL, as he rode well in advance of his big ship-ping herd, had an uneasy feeling he was in for trouble when he spotted the dust cloud boiling up against the northern sky.

"Horses," he told his range boss, Sime Dobie, "several of them and coming fast. Tell the boys to get set, but don't start anything till I give the word. Maybe we can talk our way out of whatever happens and that's better than shooting our way out."

Dobie, a taciturn individual, merely nodded He turned his horse and ambled back along the marching column of the herd to warn the point, swing, flank and drag riders. Back of the drag accompanying the remuda of spare horses and the chuck wagons, were seven men Wardell held in reserve against possible trouble. Dobie planned to swing them to the front at once. With his reserve hands riding beside him he circled the herd and back to where Wardell still paced his horse slowly forward.

"Bunch 'em and hold 'em," Dobie shouted to the point men as he swept past.

The point men instantly got busy. Before Dobie had reined in beside the boss they had the leaders milling, the following cows jostling to a halt. The task was not difficult because the cattle were glad of the chance to crop the tall and rich grass.

Meanwhile the dust cloud had rolled much nearer. A few minutes later Wardell could distinguish the bouncing dots beneath it that were horsemen.

"Four fellers," he remarked. "Well, glad it ain't more. We can handle four without any trouble."

"Maybe," replied Dobie.

"Chances are that feller we saw riding the base of the hills yesterday morning and keeping cases on us rode on ahead to tell the others we were coming this way," said Wardell.

"Maybe," Dobie replied.

"Chances are there won't be anything come of it we can't talk ourselves out of," Wardell observed hopefully.

"Maybe," Dobie monotoned for a third time.

Wardell turned on him irritably. Dang it! Can't you ever say anything but 'maybe'?" he snorted.

"Maybe," Dobie replied.

Old Tom rumbled like a fly pestered steer and turned his attention to the approaching riders.

Larger and larger grew the speeding horses. The riders took definite form. Wardell noted sagging sixguns, rifle stocks protruding from saddle boots.

"Loaded for bear, all right," he muttered. "Well, we'll see what's what in another ten minutes."

At a distance of nearly five hundred yards the horsemen pulled up. Then one raised his hand, palm outward, in the universal gesture of peace and rode slowly forward alone. As he drew near the Flying W owner and his hands gave him a careful once-over.

He was a man of medium height, sturdily built, broad of shoulder. Of his face little could be seen except the glint of dark eyes in the shadow of his low-drawn hatbrim and a bristle of black beard that grew high on his cheek bones. Reining in his horse at three or four paces he nodded.

"Howdy," he said.

"Howdy," Wardell returned.

"Nueces country?" the man asked.

"That's right," Wardell admitted. "We're from the Nueces country."

The other's eyes narrowed slightly. "Well," he said, "that being the case you've come far enough."

"Why?" Wardell asked, although he knew perfectly well what the answer would be.

"Because," the other said, "we don't aim to have our range infected with the Spanish fever you got down there. We've got improved stock up here and you know what the fever does to shorthorns."

Wardell regarded him a minute, his jaw tightening. "Listen," he said at length, "I've got seventeen Nueces cowhands with me and they ain't exactly a Sunday School gathering. "And," he added pointedly, "I don't notice but four of you fellers."

"Uh-huh, reckon that's so," the bearded man agreed. "Uh-huh, you don't notice but four, and I'll tell you why. Us fellers figured you wouldn't be apt to start gunning just four gents riding up for a palaver, so just four came along."

He paused a moment, then finished his speech with grim finality. "But—there are fifty-some gents holed up farther along, waiting. Uh-huh, holed up with saddle guns. If us fellers don't happen to ride back to report, or if they see those cows rolling along, well, reckon you can guess the rest without over-straining your think tank."

Wardell could guess, without an excessive expenditure of brain power. "There's no fever in this herd and no ticks to drop off and infect your feeding and bedding grounds," he declared. "Every one of my cows was dipped, inspected and cleared before they left the Nueces country. Besides, most of these cows are improved stuff, too. We're no danger to you, feller."

"Maybe," the other returned, employing Dobie's favorite word, "but we ain't taking no chances. Why didn't you use the east route like the other herds do?"

Wardell flushed and looked uncomfortable. "Those—those herds pack fever ticks," he muttered.

The other's bearded lips opened in a raucous laugh. "Uh-huh, makes considerable difference whose steer gets a horn in him, don't it?" he jeered. "You don't want to take the east route 'cause you're scared of tick fever! But you want us fellers to take the risk with your cows so you can get through easy, eh?"

Wardell flushed still more. He was a fair man and had to admit the force of the argument. He tried another tack.

"Listen, feller," he pleaded, "you're a cowman and you know if a cowman can't get his stock to market he's sunk. Suppose you send men here to inspect my herd? I'm willing to take the chance."

The other considered a moment, then shook his head. "The boys would never stand for it," he said. "We got some mighty mule-headed members hereabouts. They'd 'low they were still taking a risk. But wait a minute till I'm finished. Us fellers don't want to make anybody trouble. We believe in live and let live. We just aim to protect ourselves and you can't blame us for that. So I'm here to lend you a hand. You can't go over our range and that's all there is to it. If you try to you'll none of you ever see the Nueces again. But there's a way you can head north. It'll take you two, maybe three days out of your way but you can get through easy enough and not cross our range."

"How's that?" Wardell asked eagerly, grasping at any straw offered.

"By way of Skull Canyon, over to the west about seven miles," the bearded man replied. "Skull Canyon is nigh twenty miles long and it runs more west than north. When you come out the other end you'll be way west of our holdings and on a section of state land where there ain't no spreads as yet. From there you can shoot for the Red River and the Crossings or on into the Panhandle or wherever you're headed for. No trouble to get through the canyon. It's a straight shoot and all you have to do is stick to the main gulch."

Wardell hated to lose the time and to submit his stock to the extra fifty or sixty miles of weight-lessening trudge, but he reluctantly admitted to himself that he had no choice.

"Okay," he said, "but how are we going to find that infernal canyon?"

"I'll show you the way," the other volunteered. 'Plumb ready to do all I can to help a feller out."

"Much obliged," Wardell replied. "We're ready to move whenever you are."

The bearded man turned in his saddle, cupped his hands to his mouth. "All right!" he shouted to his distant companions. "They're willing to take the canyon trail. I'll guide 'em there. You fellers ride back and tell the boys everything is okay. Be seeing you later."

The three waiting riders waved their hands, whirled their horses and rode back the way they had come.

"All right," said the bearded man, "let's go. Turn your critters due west toward those hills over there. The canyon runs through a spur that shoots out this way a mite to the north."

It was easy going across the level plains of the lower Panhandle where a "trail" was mostly wherever a horseman chose to ride. The herd made good speed and the afternoon was still early when the dark mouth of the canyon came into view.

Skull Canyon is not and never was a nice place. Winding through the Salado Hills, it is a gateway to the north. The whole terrain, jagged, torn, abysmal, gives the appearance of having been clove by stroke on stroke of lightning in the course of some awful natural convulsion when the world was young. Comanche, Apache and those who came before them struggled in its depths and left their bones as mute witnesses to the bitterness of the conflict. Smuggler bands and outlaws fought bloody battles in the shadow of its walls and towering slopes. Sheepmen and cattlemen added a sanguinary chapter to its history.

The men killed in Skull Canyon were for the most part left unburied. Coyotes and buzzards picked their bones. The ants cleaned and polished them. The hot Texas sun bleached them white. Fragments and shards lie scattered in the scant grass or moulder under clumps of bush. A rider threading the gorge at night when it is damp can scarce repress a shudder, hardy though he may be, when a small and wan glow greets his eyes, for he knows that the ghostly glimmer emanates from a skull.

So it is small wonder that Tom Wardell hung back a trifle, mentally, when the bearded man with a wave of his hand indicated the shadowy opening between its pillars of black stone. An aura of tragedy seemed to rise from the shadowy depths like a miasma from a swamp, sensed though not seen. Wardell didn't know why he should feel that way about it, but he did.

"There she is," said the bearded man, "a straight shoot to the north and west. All you got to do is keep to the main canyon. Don't turn off sideways anywhere or you'll get lost. Just keep ambling ahead, north by west, and you can't miss coming out on the open prairie at the other end. Then it's easy going up into the Panhandle or to the Red. *Adios!*"

He whirled his horse and with another derisive wave of his hand sped back east, leaving Tom Wardell more than a little uncomfortable.

"That hellion seemed to be enjoying some sort of a joke," he growled to Dobie. "Wonder if he figures to get us lost in that hole?"

"Don't reckon there's much danger of that," returned the range boss. "After all, we've been around a mite, Tom, and it's just as woolly down in the lower Nueces and over to the Big Bend as it can be up here. What did he say his name was?"

"Darned if I know," replied Wardell. "Come to think of it, I don't believe he said. Oh, the devil with him! Let's go!"

The herd rolled forward and entered the gorge. Once inside, despite its sinister appearance, the going was easy. The floor was level with few boulders and scant vegetation. Care had to be taken to prevent the cows from straying into the side canyons where there was water and good grass, but no other difficulties were encountered. Wardell began to develop a more cheerful outlook. After all, it was better to lose a few days of time and a few pounds off the cows than to risk a rukus in which somebody might have been killed.

A few miles inside the canyon the bore began bending more to the west and to narrow slightly. The walls were not high, scarcely more than sixty feet to the rimrock, but above stretched long, steep slopes, benched and ridged, to the distant jagged skyline.

The curve sharpened somewhat, snaked around a bulge of cliff. Ahead the way was clear, the canyon marching between its low walls and dizzy slopes. The rimrock was clothed with chaparral growth that was but a shallow fringe on the lip of the wall, where erosion and crumbling had provided a scanty film of soil and deep crevices into which roots could thrust. The low lying sun glinted on the leaves and twigs. Nothing moved. The silence was unbroken.

And then without any preliminary warning a roar of gunfire burst from the silent growth. Two point men went down to lie without sound or motion. Another crash of shots and one of the swingmen whirled from his saddle. Bullets stormed about the drag and the chuck wagons, which were just rounding the bulge. Before Wardell and Dobie realized what was happening the second swing rider was sprawled on the ground.

The flank men spun their horses about and streaked back toward the rear of the herd through a hail of lead. A man yelled with pain as a slug drilled his arm. Another clutched at his blood-gushing cheek.

"Back!" yelled the quick-witted Dobie. "Back around the bulge! We're drygulched!"

The Flying W hands needed no urging. Bending low in the hulls they sent their mounts scudding for cover. Back of the sheltering bulge they pulled up, fuming and cursing.

"The snake-blooded hellions!" stormed Wardwell. "So this is why they wanted us to slide into this hole—so they could gun the bunch of us. Just wait!"

Dismounting, he stole forward cautiously, endeavoring to reach a point where he could peer around the cliff. But the instant his head showed a bullet fanned his face, followed by a bee-buzzing flock of the things. Wardell ducked and swore.

"They're holed up in the bushes," he told Dobie. "There ain't a chance of us sliding around and getting the range. Come on, we'll ride back and circle through the hills and get behind them."

"We'll get lost sure as shooting," protested Dobie, but nevertheless he followed the owner's lead.

But not for far. They had covered barely a hundred yards when lead stormed around them and sent them scurrying back to the bulge.

"They can see a long ways down the canyon from where they're perched," Dobie pointed out. "There ain't nothing for us to do but hole up here and wait for dark. Slide the chuck wagons and the remuda in under this overhang and line the boys up watching in every direction. They can't root us out of here, anyhow, and soon as it gets dark enough we'll slide up there and see what's what. We'll be on an equal footing with them then. Reckon they slipped a mite. Figured to get us all before we could do a thing. Must have overlooked this cliff and the cover it gives us."

Wardell swore, fuming with rage and impatience, but was forced to admit the wisdom of Dobie's plan.

"Be dark early," the range boss commented, "clouds banking up heavy in the west. Liable to be rain, too."

The sky was indeed darkening but the hours passed slowly for the group huddled under the shelter of the overhang. The canyon was deathly still.

"The cows must have strayed quite a ways," Dobie remarked. "Don't hear a sound of 'em."

Finally full dark descended. Under cover of the gloom the Flying W bunch stole up the gorge. The sky was heavily overcast but a wan glow filled the canyon's depths. They found the bodies of the slain riders, but although they crept forward for some distance they discovered no trace of the cattle.

After considerable searching Dobie discovered a way up the cliff to the rimrock. With the greatest caution they mounted to the crest and prowled about through the growth, and found nothing. They returned to the overhang, mounted their horses and, leaving a guard to look after the wagons and the remuda, rode up the canyon. Mile after mile they covered through a rain that was steadily growing heavier, and again found nothing.

"Those cows never strayed this far," Dobie declared with decision. "Tom, those hellions run 'em off."

Wardell had already arrived at a similar conclusion, but he swore bitterly and forged on.

Finally, weary, soaking wet, disgusted and miserable, they took dubious shelter under another overhang, managed to get a fire going and a little fitful sleep. The gray light of dawn found them in the saddle again, riding past the dark mouths of side canyons and fissures.

"The devils could have slid 'em into any of these holes," said Wardell, "and there's no trailing them after that rain, but come on, I want to see what's the other side of this gulch."

After more miles of riding they reached the north mouth of the canyon. Beyond rolled mile after mile of fertile rangeland, lonely, deserted, shimmering green and gold in the morning sunlight.

Tom Wardell's face had set in vindictive lines. There was a look about his mouth that Dobie knew well as he turned and shook his fist to the east.

"Four good men done in and three thousand prime beefs run off!" he muttered. "The snake-blooded, murdering cow-thieves! Fine lot of sidewinders live in this section. They want war, eh? Well, they'll get it. Come on, I want to take a look at that creek over there."

Dobie and the others followed in silence. They knew that Wardell was formulating some deep-seated plan, a plan that meant trouble for somebody. Tom Wardell was a black Scotchman by descent. If he never forgot a favor, he likewise never forgot a wrong. His blood was feudin' blood, as he had been that of his Highland forbears. To Tom Wardell, vengeance was a personal prerogative. Forgiveness was an abstract something indulged in by the weakling.

For several miles they rode north, following the course of the stream. Finally Wardell drew rein at the foot of a rise. To the east were swales and ridges well grown with thick brush. To the north and west the prairie rolled on, still lonely and deserted, rich in grass, with ample water. Wardell surveyed the scene in silence for some moments. Then he turned to Dobie.

"Sime," he said, "we're coming back up here. Uh-huh, we're coming back to stay. It's good range. The Flying W is headed for a new stamping ground. I'm sick of that danged Nueces country anyhow, with its heat and its droughts. Uh-huh, we're moving. All right, back into that infernal canyon and get the wagons rolling south."

He turned and again shook his clenched fist toward the east.

"War they want, eh?" he repeated. "I'll give 'em war!"

A little more than two months later a great trail herd of many thousand head rolled slowly northward toward the shadow of the Salado Hills. It travelled mostly by night and under cover of darkness it entered Skull Canyon. Behind it rumbled many wagons and with it rode nearly a hundred men armed to the teeth.

For Tom Wardell had persuaded several of his neighbors to join him in the northward trek to a new range.

In the light of morning the herd and its appurtenances and alert guards forged from the north mouth of Skull Canyon. At its head, his face grim with purpose, rode Tom Wardell.

"I'll give 'em war!" he muttered.

CHAPTER SIX

O LD TOM CEASED SPEAKING and sat gazing at Slade through the haze of cigarette smoke.

"So you see now, son, why I ain't got no use for that nest of sidewinders over to the east of here," he concluded.

"Yes," Slade replied thoughtfully, "I can understand why you would harbor a grievance, but there are a few little points I'd like to have cleared up, if you don't mind. I believe you said you saw somebody keeping tabs on you the day before the man with the beard stopped you?"

"That's right," agreed Wardell.

Slade nodded. "We'll pass that for a minute," he said. "Just how did the man who stopped you know you were from the Nueces country? Lots of country between here and the Nueces—the Brazos, the Colorado, the Trinity, and so on. Your herd might have come from any one of those sections. And yet he at once asked you if you weren't from the Nueces. Looks like somebody had been keeping tab on you for quite a while, perhaps ever since or before you left the Nueces."

Old Tom tugged his mustache and conceded it looked a bit that way.

"Getting back to my first question," Slade resumed. "Somebody was keeping tabs on you twenty-four hours before you were stopped. Before you were stopped, did you pass any cattle?"

"Yes, quite a few, several different brands," Wardell admitted.

"Which meant you were well onto the pastures of the folks over to the east," Slade pointed out. "And if your concentration is correct and the fellow keeping tabs on you was from up here, they allowed at least a full day to pass by before they stopped you. Allowed you to get well onto their feeding grounds. Every cattleman knows that the danger of Spanish fever comes from ticks dropping off infected cows and fastening onto other cows that use the feeding grounds. And still they let you come onto their grassland before they stopped you."

"I've got the answer to that," old Tom exclaimed triumphantly. "They weren't scared of fever. They were just figuring a way to wideloop my herd."

"Doubtless," Slade admitted, "but the way you interpret it presupposes that everybody in the section, including the law enforcement officers, was in on the deal, which doesn't seem exactly reasonable. There are a dozen or more ranches to the south and east of here. I've been around a bit and I've never encountered a section where all the owners and their associates would combine to perpetrate a widelooping and drygulching. All in all, it looks to me like that whiskered gent and his friends were the only ones who knew you were headed this way, and I'd say they had known it for a long time, perhaps even before you started your big shipping herd on the trail."

"Say," Wardell growled, "are you trying to make out a case for those hellions over east?"

"I'm not trying to make out a case for anybody," Slade replied quietly. "I'm just calling to your attention a few peculiar angles connected with the affair and trying to show how strange that bearded man's story sounds and how it doesn't tie up with his actions. Does it really look like that man was acting for the whole section up here? Does it look like the rest of the folks up here had any notion you and your herd were this side of the Brazos?"

Old Tom rumbled, swore, tugged at his mustache and glared at the Ranger with what would have been, were not the matter under discussion so deadly serious, a really amusing expression of personal injury. Sime Dobie chuckled. Young Tom grinned, and winced with the pain inflicted on his sore jaw. Dolores smiled at Slade, who smiled back.

"Mr. Wardell, have you been losing cows?" he asked suddenly.

"Yes, plenty of 'em, and so have my neighbors I brought up here with me," the rancher replied, "but what else can you expect?"

"Folks over to the east have also been losing cows," Slade commented.

"That's what they say," Wardell snorted.

"Well," Slade replied, "They lost some yesterday. I saw a herd of Circle K stock run through that canyon yesterday. The sheriff was chasing the rustlers and a bunch was holed up on the rimrock waiting to blow him from under his hat, at right the same place they laid for you."

Briefly he recounted the incident of Skull Canyon the day before.

Old Tom stared. He got up and paced the floor, tugging his mustache and rumbling.

"Dad blame you!" he exclaimed in injured tones, "you got me all worked up and bothered. I wish I'd never laid eyes on you."

"Sit down, Mr. Wardell, I have something to tell you," Slade said.

Old Tom resumed his chair and Slade continued. "Mr. Wardell, the description you give of the man who stopped you tallies pretty well with the description of a notorious outlaw it is said has been operating near this section for the past few months, a fellow who calls himself Ellis Dawson. He started plenty of trouble over around Doan's Crossing a couple of years back. The Rangers caught up with his bunch and wiped out most of them but Dawson and one or two more escaped. The drygulching that was pulled on you and the one attempted on the sheriff were remarkably reminiscent of the methods he employed.

I heard he was operating to the north and east of here, but it's beginning to look like he may have moved down here. By the way, have you seen that man who stopped you since you came up here last?"

"No, I haven't," old Tom admitted, "and I sure wanted to meet up with that hellion again. When we first came here, before the sidewinders over to the east knew we were here to stay, we scouted around quite a bit trying to locate that gent, but we never found a whisker of him, and nobody 'peared to have ever seen him or heard of him, or if they did they wouldn't admit it."

"I see," Slade remarked thoughtfully. "Well, what do you think?"

"Tarnation! I don't know what to think," old Tom admitted. "All I know is that you've got me all bothered and confused."

"You've never associated with any of your neighbors to the east?" Slade asked abruptly.

"No, except for one feller who came up here just a little while before we did," Wardell ansewered. "Feller named Carter Renshaw. He's got a spread right over to the east and a bit north of our holdings. We pass by his ranchhouse on the way to Plaino, where we do our buying. Somehow he doesn't strike me as being a bad sort. Hasn't been in the section long enough to get contaminated, I reckon. He's been over here once or twice."

Slade nodded and stood up, smiling down at them from his great height. "Well, reckon I'll be riding back to town," he said. "Thanks for everything, it's been nice to talk with all of you."

After Slade had ridden away, old Tom sat silent for a few minutes. Suddenly he jumped to his feet. "I want to talk to Manuel," he said. "The rest of you wait here till I come back."

The old cook was cleaning up. He nodded to the boss.

"Manuel," Wardell said, "you 'peared to know that feller Slade who just left. Who is he?"

"*Patron*," the old Mexican replied, "he is the friend of the lowly, the champion of the oppressed, the comforter of all who know fear or doubt or sorrow. He is a strange man, *Patron*. Where trouble is he appears and when he has departed the trouble has also departed and behind is left peace and content. He is hated by the evil, loved by others. He has killed men, but only as an act of justice. Yes, I know him—I have seen him before—and I know of his deeds."

Wardell went back to the living room. He fixed his eyes on Dobie. 'Sime," he said, "you been acting sort of funny for the past couple of hours, almost like you know that big jigger or know of him."

"Yep," Dobie replied," I know what he's called and I know something about his reputation, one way or the other. I spotted him the minute I laid eyes on him. Saw him once before over in the Big Bend country, and when you see him once you don't forget him. He's called El Halcon by the folks down around the Rio Grande—The Hawk. Looks sort of like one, doesn't he? One of those big gray-eyed mountain devils that'll take on an eagle. There are plenty of folks will tell you he's got the fastest gun-hand in the whole dang Southwest. And there are some scattered around who'll tell you that if he isn't an owlhoot he misses being one by the skin of his teeth."

Dobie paused. Old Tom looked at him suspiciously. "That all you got to tell about him?" he asked.

"Well," Dobie replied, "if there's anything more to tell, I reckon he'll tell you when he's of a mind to."

Old Tom glowered. He felt pretty sure that Dobie wasn't telling all he knew, but he also knew perfectly well that there was no making him talk till he was good and ready. He turned to young Tom.

"And what do you think about him?" he asked.

"Well, Dad," young Tom replied, "I'll tell you. He nigh to busted my jaw and made me look feather-headed, but just the same I think he's a man to ride the river with."

Old Tom did not contradict the highest compliment the rangeland can pay. He glanced at Dolores.

"And what do you think?" he demanded truculently.

"The kind of a man a girl dreams about but never expects to see," his daughter returned sweetly.

Old Tom threw out his hands despairingly. "Oh, what the devil's the use!" he snorted. "That hellion's got the whole shebang hypnotized!"

Abruptly a grin stretched his lips and made his bad-tempered old face wonderfully youthful and pleasing.

"But I'm as loco as the rest of you," he said. "Tarnation! I like him, too!"

"Shall I send somebody down to take over the chore of guarding the trail?" Dobie asked.

"Oh, the devil with it!" growled the boss. "That feller might take a notion to ride back again, and I don't want any more busted jaws hereabouts."

CHAPTER SEVEN

S LADE FELT HE HAD ACCOMPLISHED SOMETHING by his trip to the Flying W. If nothing else, he had gotten old Tom Wardell a bit uncertain and worried. He didn't think that Wardell in his present frame of mind would do anything to start a row with his neighbors to the east. Which was all to the good. The unexpected conditions he had encountered had bothered him no little. They had the makings of a bad range war, which in turn would mean trouble for Captain McNelty. If such a row got going good, Captain Jim would be forced to send more men into the section, men he could ill spare at the time. Slade made up his mind that Captain Jim wouldn't have this problem to put up with. He hoped and believed he would be able to influence the cowmen of the other faction as he had Wardell. But that chore was secondary to the chore that brought him into the section. Rather, it was an outgrowth, or so he believed, of the machinations of the outlaw Ellis Dawson; for Slade was very much of the opinion that the bearded man Tom Wardell had encountered was no other than Dawson. Wardell's rather sketchy description of Dawson lined up pretty well with other equally vague descriptions proffered by people who saw or claimed to have seen the outlaw leader. And Slade shrewdly suspected that the beard was grown or donned by Dawson for the express purpose of centering attention on an individual who doubtless looked greatly different without it. Some men can grow a beard very fast, and even a well made and properly secured false beard would fool the casual observer. So Slade felt that he should not concentrate on looking for a man with a black beard.

But just who to look for he had not the slightest notion. He hadn't forgotten Bob Biggers' wet boots, but he was forced to admit that Biggers coud have been digging out a waterhole the day before, and Biggers impressed him as the sort of an individual who would get down and work with his men rather than issue orders from the sidelines.

However, at present Biggers was all he had that in the least resembled a suspect. Doubtless that lack could be remedied by getting better acquainted with the dwellers in the section.

Pondering the problem, he sent Shadow scrambling up the break in the canyon wall to the rimrock.

The trail left by the fleeing drygulchers was nearly twenty-four hours old and not easy to follow, but they had left enough evidence of their passing to guide the trained eyes of El Halcon. A broken twig, an overturned boulder, a faint hoof print on a patch of softer soil. Slade followed the trail as it curved west by south through the gorge that finally opened out onto the grassland, as he suspected it would. Here he pulled up shaking his head.

"A herd of buffalo wouldn't leave a track here," he told Shadow.

Quite some distance to the southeast Slade spotted a considerable number of cattle. They were scattered in a roughly circular formation.

"Those gents were riding mighty fast and it's just about certain they didn't draw rein till they were out of the canyon, and it was a hot day," he told Shadow, "and horses have to drink."

After a rather lengthy period of riding, for distances are deceptive on the Staked Plains, he drew near the cattle. As he suspected, they were clumped in the vicinity of a large waterhole from which ran a little trickle of overflow. Dismounting, he carefully examined the banks of the hole. Mingling with the hoof marks of the cattle were the prints of horses' irons, and Slade was certain the prints were not more than twenty-four hours old.

He discovered more. Plain to his keen and experienced eyes was the direction in which the horses had been turned when they had finished drinking, and across the softer and almost bar rim of the hole the prints headed east by north.

Across the Staked Plains, men most always ride in a straight line to reach an objective; there is nothing to be gained by making detours for all the soil is alike where there are no steep slopes, no hollows and no broken ground to be avoided. He triangulated the waterhole with the hills to the north and the long, straight hypotenuse of the triangle was the course he followed. And as he suspected, after little more than half an hour of riding at an easy pace he sighted the dark mouth of Skull Canyon.

Slade was positive that five horses drank at the waterhole the day before. With this in mind he tried in every way possible as he rode to ascertain if the gang had split up, one party heading for Skull Canyon, the other for some place else, doubtless the town of Lucas. But here all his experience and sagacity were of no avail. The prairie grass showed no sign of a passing hoof and the stony floor of the canyon mouth was likewise barren of results.

But if it had really been Bob Biggers and his men staging the drygulching on the canyon rim, they must have separated somewhere, two riding off while Biggers and two others entered the canyon, very likely with the notion of providing an excellent alibi for themselves.

Finally he gave up in disgust and remounted. Hooking one long leg over the saddle horn he rolled a cigarette and considered the situation.

"I reckon what we should have done yesterday was shoot off a couple of hats instead of tree branches," he complained to Shadow. "That's the system the smart range detective employs, or so they say. Shoot off the hats, retrieve them and then confront the villain with a rainshed with his name or initials on the sweatband, and everything is lovely. Of course, there's a catch or two in it. When you drill a hat at six hundred yards there's always a mighty good chance of drilling the head under it, too. Then if you got the right jigger, everything is fine and you don't need the hat. If you make a mistake, then you've spoiled a head as well as a hat. Which sometimes is inconvenient. Take this morning, for instance, I could have plugged young Tom Wardell through the back and have had apparent justification for so doing, but afterward I'd have been sorry. Would be a shame to kill a jigger with as nice and pretty a sister as he's got. So I guess we'll just stick to our usual methods. Maybe we can manage to stay in one piece and perhaps get a break somehow that will straighten things out. Head for town, horse, I'm getting hungry again and there isn't much of anything here for even an old grassburner like yourself. June along!"

It was well after dark when Slade reached Lucas. After stabling Shadow he repaired to the First Chance for something to eat. The big saloon was already getting pretty well crowded and there was every indication that a hilarious night was in the offering.

"Pay day for the spreads," the waiter who took Slade's order told him. "The boys will be feeling their oats before morning. Right now ain't nothing to what's coming."

Before he had finished his dinner Slade was of the opinion that the waiter had the right idea. The place was filling up and the patrons growing livelier by the minute. The majority were undoubtedly cowboys from the spreads to the east and south, but there were certain individuals who interested Slade. Dressed in rangeland garb and undoubtedly familiar with the cattle business though they were, Slade doubted if they had had any recent familiarity with rope or branding iron. He had gathered from Sheriff Sloan that Lucas was a focal point for riders from all over so it was logical to assume that questionable characters would appear.

Slade agreed with the sheriff that the Panhandle was the coming cattleland of Texas. Herds were pouring in from the overcrowded pastures of the Trinity, the Brazos, the Nueces and elsewhere. Here, what early explorers had called "The Great American Desert" was a vast expanse of finest grassland, millions of acres rich in Buffalo grass, needle and wheat and curly mesquite. Land that could be acquired at a very low price. Cowmen were beginning to realize this and to take advantage of the opportunity presented.

The coming of more and more cattle meant that opportunities for the lawless were also increasing and the section was ideally suited to widelooping, with hills to the west and beyond, the wasteland of the Tucumari Desert, with the mountains of New Mexico and ready markets for stolen cows conveniently at hand. Also, communities were springing into being, which meant banks, stage lines and railroad lines that provided more rich pickings for the unscrupulous. And it was still a land of great distances, far from centers of population, still a land where the law of the sixshooter was to a large extent the only law.

So it was not particularly surprising that such a character as Ellis Dawson should set up in business here, considerably to the south and west of where he had been last reported.

Of course the presence of Dawson in the section was predicated on the assumption that old Tom Wardell had told a straight story. Wardell had made out a pretty good case for himself, which was to be expected, he had been doing the talking, but Slade was of the opinion that in the main Wardell's account was valid. He could be mistaken, of course, but he did not credit Wardell with enough imagination to concoct such a yarn. He had catalogued Wardell as a stubborn and vindictive old shorthorn who it would be hard to pry loose from an opinion but who was intelligent enough to change his notions if he felt it was to his advantage to do so.

The keen-eyed, alert Sime Dobie, Wardell's range boss, was something of an enigma. Slade had not missed Dobie's amused expression during his stay at the Flying W ranchhouse and he wondered just how much the little range boss knew or suspected.

Well, that could bide for the time being. He dismissed the matter and as he ate gave his attention to what was going on around him. A few minutes later Bob Biggers came in with the two cowboys who had accompanied him the night before. He waved his hand to Slade and continued to the far end of the bar, apparently his favorite spot. He had hardly got settled with a glass in his hand when Carter Renchaw arrived, not alone this time, but with five men trailing behind him, alert, capable looking men and all young. Slade noted that they shot searching glances around the room as they entered. They also made their way to the end of the bar near where Bob Biggers and his two hands were drinking.

Slade had finished his meal and was smoking a cigarette when Sheriff Sloan showed up, spotted him and came over to the table. He drew up a chair and gave his order to a waiter.

"Well, what you been doing with yourself all day?" he asked the Ranger.

"Took a ride up to the Flying W, old Tom Wardell's place," Slade replied.

The sheriff stared. "And you didn't get shot?"

"Not quite," Slade admitted with a smile.

The sheriff shook his head. "Don't understand it," he said. "That bunch sure doesn't usually hanker for visitors and lets anybody coming around know it."

"Possible for them to change their minds," Slade pointed out.

"Yes, reckon that's so, under certain circumstances," the sheriff agreed. Abruptly he fixed Slade with his gaze.

"Feller, don't get me wrong, but I'm going to ask you a question," he said. "As sheriff of the county I have to sort of keep tabs on things and on folks."

"Shoot!" Slade said smilingly. He had a pretty good notion what was coming.

"What I want to know," the sheriff said slowly, "is did that bunch up there bring you in to do their gun-slinging for them?"

"Funny," Slade replied with another smile, "that's just about what Tom Wardell asked me, did the folks over here bring me in as a hired gunhand. I'll give you the same answer as I gave Wardell."

"And that is..." prompted the sheriff.

"No!" Slade said shortly.

"Nobody brought me here," he added, "and, nobody's going to tell me when to leave."

The sheriff got the implication and flushed a little. "Didn't have any such notion in mind," he disavowed. "I don't ask anybody to move along if they behave themselves."

"Keep that in mind—later," Slade said, without explaining.

The waiter brought his order and Sheriff Sloan addressed himself to his food, while Slade sat smoking and watching the activities around him. The sheriff took a swallow of coffee and spoke.

"Suppose old Tom told you that yarn about him being drygulched and losing cows when he was up this way the first time," he remarked.

"I'm not so sure it's altogether a yarn," Slade replied quietly.

Sheriff Sloan looked skeptical. "Why?" he asked.

"I believe that Wardell claims four of his men were killed in the course of the row," Slade answered. "Well, if you'd ridden a little farther up Skull Canyon yesterday you would have seen four graves with the grass just starting to grow on them."

The sheriff stared. "And you believe his yarn?" he asked incredulously.

"Yes, I do," Slade replied quietly. "I don't give him credit for being able to make it up. By the way, how did you learn about the story?"

"Why, he told Carter Renshaw and Renshaw sort of spread the thing around," Sloan explained. "Fact is, I believe Renshaw believes it, too."

"Last night when we were discussing the Nueces bunch you didn't mention that Renshaw was acquainted with the Nueces people," Slade remarked pointedly. "You intimated that he'd ust spoken with some of the younger hands who rode past his place."

Sheriff Sloan flushed again. "I was just sort of trying to feel you out," he admitted, "wanted to know if you had any leanings toward that bunch. You see, you just sort of rode in here from nowhere and right off got mixed up in a shindig. I ain't saying anything against you, Slade, but you'll have to admit you've sort of got the look of a two-gun quick-draw man and I do have to keep an eye on that sort. Been getting too danged many of late."

Slade's eyes danced with laughter. "Sloan," he said, "you're pretty young for your job and, I'd say, rather inexperienced, but I've a notion you'll improve. If you manage to live long enough," he added a bit grimly. "Barging head-on into things and jumping at conclusions is not the way to do it."

The sheriff looked a bit uncomfortable and then admitted frankly, "You may have something there."

Slade had been watching Bob Biggers and Carter Renshaw standing together at the far end of the bar. The two men appeared to be arguing about something, and the argument was steadily growing more heated. Renshaw spoke in a cool, quiet voice, Biggers in a grating rumble, his huge hands gesturing angrily.

Abruptly the climax came. Biggers bawled a curse and launched a blow at the other's face. Renshaw stepped back lithely and Biggers' ponderous fist missed its mark. And as he rushed forward, Renshaw's right hand shot out like the head of a striking snake; a stubby, double-barreled derringer smacked against his palm, the twin muzzles yawning hungrily at Biggers who halted as if he had run into a stone wall, gripping the butt of his gun.

Renshaw spoke, his voice carrying clearly in the sudden hush. "Biggers," he said, "I have no desire to kill you, but if you keep on the way you're going you'll force me to do so. Now go away and leave me alone."

Biggers seemed to hesitate, his face working. Sheriff Sloan leaped to his feet with a bellow of anger. He charged across the room, flinging men left and right out of his way, and displayed admirable courage but very poor judgment as he stepped squarely in front of Renshaw's levelled gun.

"Renshaw! Put up that iron!" he shouted. "I'll have no corpse and cartridge session here. Put it up, I say!"

Renshaw eyed him coolly a moment. Then he shrugged his broad shoulders and with a deft flip of his hand sent the stubby .41 sliding back into its sleeve holster. He turned his back on the sheriff and with a hand that didn't spill a drop raised his brimming glass to his lips. Biggers, still rumbling and muttering, sidled down the bar a ways, his two silent punchers beside him, and swallowed a drink of whiskey at a gulp. Sheriff Sloan glowered at both men a moment then returned to the table and sat down.

"Danged loco jugheads!" he fumed. "Another second and everybody would have been in on it. See what I'm up against all the time? Bad blood between those two."

Slade nodded and did not comment, for his keen eyes had noted what nobody else appeared to. The derringer with which Renshaw menaced Biggers wasn't cocked, and Slade knew that type of sleeve gun was single-action. Renshaw hadn't the slightest intention of shooting Biggers, nor did he fear that Biggers would pull on him. Otherwise he'd never have taken a chance with an uncocked gun against a fast draw. Failing to cock the derringer was just one of the little slips even a smart man will sometimes make.

Aside from that one small neglect, the act was perfect and had apparently fooled everybody except El Halcon with his uncanny facility for noting the smallest details even in moments of hectic action.

CHAPTER EIGHT

S HORTLY AFTERWARD, CARTER RENSHAW and his men left the First Chance. Bob Biggers immediately came over to the table and sat down. The sheriff eyed him belligerently.

"Well, what was the matter with you two?" he demanded.

Biggers scowled. "That horned toad was talking out of turn," he said. "He was 'lowing that those Nueces hellions didn't have anything to do with running off the Circle K herd or the other cows that have been coming up missing hereabouts during the past few months, that very likely it was a New Mexico outfit that was doing it. I pointed out to him what everybody knows, that the only way those cows could get across to the New Mexico markets for stolen beefs is north by way of Skull Canyon or some of its side holes and on across Tom Wardell's holdings. I told him there ain't no getting across the desert down here or any place less than thirty miles to the north of here. Well, one word led to another and I got so riled I took a poke at him. Missed him—the devil is quick as a cat—and that danged gambler's draw of his is chain lightning. I was just wondering if I'd better take a chance on pulling on him when you barged in."

"A good thing you didn't," growled the sheriff. "You'd be over to the coroner's office right now if you had."

Slade slid in a question voiced with casual curiosity. "You say there's no getting across the desert down here?" he asked.

"There sure ain't, not with a herd of cows," Biggers replied vigorously. "It's a two days drive for a herd and not a drop of water between here and the New Mexico mountains. A jigger on horseback and with canteens can do it if he has good luck and don't get caught in a dust storm, but not cows. It just can't be done."

Slade proceeded to draw Biggers out a bit. "I've heard that Captain Arrington of the Rangers made it across once and found water on the way," he remarked.

"Uh-huh, but you didn't hear all of it," said Biggers. "Arrington did find water, the Lost Lakes he'd heard of, but he figured they were in Gaines County a bit to the south and less than half way across the desert over here. But he got caught in a blizzard and got all mixed up as to distances and directions. Everybody knows now that the Lost Lakes are over in New Mexico and way to the south. Oh, I know folks will tell you that old-timers used to say the Indians made it across here with horses and cows and things and that they must have known where to find water, but if they did, nobody's been able to do it since their time. I believe it was just a yarn, anyhow. I tried it across there once and got about half way and decided I'd better hightail back where I come from. Shove cows across there in the blazin' heat, especially the way it is this time of the year! I tell you it's plain hell out there."

Sheriff Sloan nodded sober agreement. "It is, I know," he put in. "I was across once and before I got to the hills over there I began to figure I'd take the Big Jump. I sure didn't come back by the same way I went. I worked up north for better'n thirty miles and crossed by way of where there's some grassland and some springs. It's hell, all right."

Slade asked another question, directed at the sheriff. "And did old-timers really maintain the Indians used to cross down here?"

"That's right," nodded Sloan. "I heard my granddad tell about it. He said his dad did know some Indians who used to cross with their stock."

Biggers didn't argue the point vocally, but he cast a derisive glance at the sheriff. Slade didn't comment.

"Yes, the only way they can get 'em across is to run 'em north, and north they have to pass across those Nueces hellions' range," Biggers declared.

The sheriff looked at Slade and rubbed his chin. "They could get 'em across Wardell's range at night without being spotted," he observed.

"Uh-huh, they could, maybe," snorted Biggers.

"Understand Wardell claims to have lost cows, too," Slade remarked mildly.

Biggers' answer was a repeat of old Tom's to a similar observation anent the claims of the ranchers to the south and east of him. "He would!"

"We're not getting anywhere with this argument, so let's cut it short," broke in the sheriff. "Bob, I want you to stay away from Renshaw. I've got enough on my hands without you two getting your bristles up and making more trouble for me. Next time I'll throw you both in the calaboose for bustin' the peace. I mean it!"

Biggers apparently believed the sheriff did mean it, for he grunted and changed the subject.

"I'm going to the bar for another drink," he said. "I'll send over a couple."

Sheriff Sloan watched him lumber across the room and shook his head. "Bob's all right, only he gets on the prod too danged quick," he observed. "Say! things are getting lively, aren't they?"

"Harmless enough so long as it's this way," commented the sheriff. "Later, when the redeye really gets to working there's liable to be some high jinks. Usually nothing overly serious, though, a busted head or two, some bloody noses and a few black eyes. I don't mind so long as nobody starts to pull something really bad, like what Renshaw and Biggers came nigh to doing. Well, I think I'll mosey around and give the other joints a once-over, just in case."

"And I think I'll head for bed," Slade replied. "It's long past midnight."

"Not a bad notion, wish I could," said Sloan. With a nod he left the saloon. Slade smoked another cigarette and then followed his example.

However, Slade did not go to bed. Instead, he quietly got the rig on Shadow and left town by way of deserted side streets and headed west. He felt pretty sure his departure had not been noticed, but just the same once he was clear of the town his voice rang out, "Trail, Shadow, trail!"

Instantly the great black extended himself. He snorted joyously, slugged his head about the bit and literally poured his long body over the ground, his flashing irons drumrolling the hard trail.

For several miles Slade sent him streaking at top speed, then he slowed down with a chuckle, confident that if anybody had attempted to follow they would have been left far behind. He rode on at a good pace, frequently glancing over his shoulder and on rises pulling up for a moment to study the back trail. It still wanted a couple of hours till dawn when he reached Skull Canyon. He forced Shadow through the growth till he reached a little open space close to the east wall, where grass grew and there was a trickle of water. There he got the rig off the black so he could graze in comfort. Then, the night being warm, he curled up on the ground with his saddle for a pillow and slept soundly till sunup.

Full daylight found him on the move. He wanted to explore the side canyons leading west from Skull and proceeded to do so. For hours he examined the numerous "coyote holes" with no results. The morning was getting along when he finally hit on a narrow gorge that showed indubitable traces of cattle passing that way no very great time before.

"Looks like this might be it," he told Shadow. "Now let's see where it goes."

Although the gorge was deathly still and Slade did not really anticipate trouble of any kind he rode warily, constantly scanning the terrain ahead and keeping a sharp watch on his surroundings.

The gorge ran almost straight in a westerly direction. Its walls were sheer and there were no side canyons. If cows had passed this way, and Slade was convinced they had, they would have had to keep on going straight ahead. There was no turning off.

Here to the north the range of hills was broader and nearly two hours had passed before he reached the west mouth of the bore. It opened onto grassland with far to the west the gray shimmer of the desert and beyond the flat-topped mountains of New Mexico lying like a shadow against the skyline.

Following the trail through the canyon had been easy, now his troubles began. The grass retained no sign of the passage of either horses or cows and there was no way to tell which direction the herd had taken. It could have turned north to reach Tom Wardell's holdings, it could have turned south or it could have continued west to the desert's edge. Slade quartered the ground with the greatest patience, covering a wide area of territory, and found nothing. Finally he gave up in disgust and sent Shadow south some distance from the hill slopes which were heavily brush grown. He had covered a few miles and had just topped the crest of a low rise when he abruptly pulled to a halt and sat gazing down the opposite sag and a little to the west.

"Shadow, that's just about the biggest one I ever saw," he remarked.

Out of the south flowed the great depression, writhing up the sags, dropping down the opposite slopes, crossing the swales, curving sharply less than a mile distant to cut almost at right angles the course he was riding, vanishing toward the gray mystery of the desert.

Fully a hundred feet wide it scored the surface of the rangeland to a depth of two yards or more, its bottom sparsely grass grown, studded with boulders, scoured out by the rushing stream that filled it in the time of heavy rains. Its sloping sides were grown with flowering weeds and succulent gramma grass, seemingly out of place here in the Panhandle. It could only have been made, Slade knew, by myriads of pounding hoofs passing and repassing during an untold number of years, hollowing out, beating down and depressing the soil. It was an old bison trail over which the vast herds used to drift from one pasture to another and back again, over and over. The great beasts would grass a section bare and then move on to another, coming back when the grass had grown again and repeating the process year after year.

Slade's black-lashed eyes narrowed a little in thought. Over there to the west was the desert. Why would the bison herds trek to the desert? Certainly they would have never attempted to cross the waterless expanse.

Slade knew that the desert had once been a lake, of which there were still several in the section, now small and mostly in a process of dessication, but that didn't answer the question. The bison trail, while old, was not old in a geological sense. The water of what had once been the lake had vanished many thousands of years before the track was made. When the first bison trod it, the desert must have been much as it was today. But the trail, to all appearances, led right on to the edge of the desert. The anomaly so intrigued him that he resolved to ride the track to the desert's edge and endeavor to find an explanation of the phenomenon. He had reached where the track began curving westward and was riding down the sloping side of the depression when he again pulled Shadow to a halt. Set near the base of the rise was a peculiar object.

It was the bleached shoulder blade of a giant bison, an enormous fan-shaped bone fourteen to sixteen inches long, ten inches wide at one end, two inches at the other. On the smooth face of this white "blackboard" of the Plains were drawings in yellow, green and red. Near the left edge of the bone two crude figures representing men were squatted beside a fire over which hung a kettle. Riding toward the camp was a single horseman. Above the figure was drawn an arrow that pointed toward what looked like a huge rock building jutting up from the smooth surface of the desert.

Slade was familiar with such signboards. He knew that the Indians used them to direct companions to a certain locality or to inform followers where they could be found. The cryptic signs, unintelligible to a white man, were plain as print to the aborigines and as easily read.

No, there was nothing unusual about the object. Slade had seen many such. But the keens eyes of El Halcon, accustomed to noting the most insignificant details, saw something that the casual observer would have very likely overlooked. He realized that one thing about the drawings was out of the ordinary. On all such guide posts he had seen the figures were dim, weathered down, for no such drawings had been made by Indians for many years. For years the bison had been gone, and with them the nomadic tribes that once roamed the Plains. Certainly none were prowling around the section at this late date. But the pigments with which the figures were drawn on this particular specimen of pseudo-aboriginee art were perfectly fresh, not weathered in the least. They had undoubtedly been daubed on the bone not more than a few months previous at the greatest.

What the blazes did it mean, Slade wondered? Who was going around painting bison shoulder blades in the fashion the Indians did, and why? He wondered if it could be some wandering cowpoke's joke. Not likely, however; cowhands didn't usually pack paint of various colors with them.

He dismounted and examined the signboard more closely. Yes, the pigments were undoubtedly fresh; his eyes had not deceived him. No great time had elapsed since they were smeared on the bleached bone. He felt that the thing carried a definite message of some kind for somebody. But it was an enigmatical message not to be read by a chance observer. The key to the whole drawing doubtless was the arrow that pointed toward what appeared to be a building out there on the arid sands where he knew perfectly well no building existed. Could be a rock formation of some kind, of course, and very likely was. The two men depicted on the bone had evidently made camp there and the grim looking block of stone no doubt had something to do with it, but having had considerable experience with desert rock formations, Slade knew that all they were likely to provide was a bit of shelter from the burning rays of the sun.

But why in blazes would anybody want to make a camp in the midst of the desolation? Men on horseback desiring to cross the desert for some reason would hardly pause. It was dangerous to attempt even at night and with full canteens. No horse could make much speed through the powdery sand and salt and alkali that was the desert's surface.

Standing behind the bone he sighted across it. If it followed the Indian tradition, the direction in which the broad blade pointed was the direction that should be followed by the traveller. All he could see was the blue shadow against the sky of a mountain far across the desert in New Mexico, and nobody needed a sign to steer for that.

He examined the drawings again, trying to read some hidden meaning from them. He knew that the colors were significant when the Indians limned out a message. In this instance the figures were done in the pale yellow, perhaps to signify that they were white men. The fire under the pot was red, as was to be expected. But why should the great block of stone be done in bright green? What did that signify, if anything? In the Indians' color-language, green stood for peaceful comfort. A devil of a place to expect to find either comfort or peace!

With a baffled mutter, he gave up, mounted Shadow and rode on toward the desert. In less than an hour he reached it. He reined in on the crest of a rise over which the bison trail dipped to flow for another five hundred yards or so and end as abruptly as though sliced off by a giant knife. Which was not strange, even did it continue across the wasteland; the constantly shifting sands quickly obliterated any track.

Far westward, many miles distant, were the shadowy outlines of the mountain range that marked the terminus of the desert, but between where Slade sat his horse and that cool shadow in the sky was a vast arid expanse fanged by chimney rocks and grotesquely carved buttes, swelling in long ridges, pocked by deep hollows, shimmering whitely in the sunlight, over its surface weaving and writhing heat devils like cosmic dancers.

Lounging comfortably in his saddle, one sinewy leg hooked over the horn, Slade rolled a cigarette and smoked thoughtfully. And as the sun sank a little and its hot beams beat obliquely on the white sands, he was suddenly entertained by Nature's most wonderful picture show, a desert mirage.

High in the sky, riding down the path of the winds, appeared a horseman, gigantic, distorted. Slade could see him bend low in his saddle, glance over his shoulder from time to time. Soundlessly the hoofs of his mount drummed the sky trail. And abruptly over the rim of the horizon appeared other horsemen, likewise huge and grotesque, a full half-dozen of them riding swiftly in pursuit. From their ranks mushroomed whitish puffs.

Rigid with suspense, his nails biting into his sweating palms, El Halcon watched the silent drama unfolding in the golden air. He saw the fleeing horseman throw up his arms, reel from his saddle and fall into limitless space; and as if his fall had snapped the cords that held in place the reflecting sky screen, the whole scene vanished and only the limitless expanse of sun drenched blue remained.

CHAPTER NINE

SLADE'S TENSE MUSCLES RELAXED, leaving him quivering as from mighty physical effort; his eyes were coldly gray, his face bleak. For he knew that what he had just witnessed was no fragment of over-wrought imagination, no fantasy of sun and air and shifting winds.

A mirage cannot lie any more than a mirror can, although as in the case of a concave or convex mirror, its images may be distorted. But if the subject standing in front of a concave mirror raises his hand, the distorted reflection in the mirror must also raise its hand. The same is true with a mirage. Any move made by its subject is faithfully portrayed in its great heat-engendered "mirror" in the sky. Somewhere over there in the white immensities, beating the sands with their horses' hoofs, rode fleshly counterparts of the ghostly horsemen who had slain a fleeing shadow with a shadowy bullet. Down there on the sands the fugitive had been a living, breathing man. The bullet that struck him down was sound and solid. The desert had reverberated to the roar of guns. Those whitish puffs had wreathed and drifted in the hot air. Even now, doubtless, the slayers were grouped around the body of their victim. Where? There was no way to tell. It could be twenty miles away or it could be seventy.

It was a killing, all right. There was no doubt in Slade's mind as to that, but he wondered what it was all about. The sheriff's posse pursuing a law breaker? It was possible, but Slade didn't think that was the answer. One thing was certain, the poor devil never had a chance.

For a long while Slade sat his horse and gazed across the weird expanse in the hope that the actors in the grim drama might appear within the range of his vision. But the wide reaches remained empty, to all appearances utterly devoid of human life. Twice more mirages formed, but each time they were the most commonplace variety, having the appearance of a large body of water rippled by the wind, reflections of the desert sands distorted by little irregularities and a small amount of turbulence in the layers of hot and cooler air that are the fundamental source of the "mirror" necessary to all mirages. Finally, with the lower edge of the sun already obscured by the distant mountain wall, he gave up, turned Shadow's head and rode east.

The most interesting angle of the episode from Slade's point of view was the indubitable fact that men were riding and acts of violence taking place somewhere out there in the deathly wasteland. And what legitimate business would anybody have on the scorching sands? That was a question Slade greatly desired the answer to. He felt that the sinister terrain was the abiding place of a mystery that would have to be solved, that in some way tied up with the lawless acts that were plaguing the section. How? He hadn't the slightest notion, but he was convinced that it was so.

It was long past dark when Slade arrived in Lucas. Repairing to the First Chance for a surrounding of chuck he found Sheriff Sloan eating a belated dinner and in a pessimistic mood.

"I'm worried," he said as Slade sat down. "There ain't anything really bad happened for two whole days."

"Doubtless that will be remedied before long," Slade told him cheerfully, adding with a touch of grimness, "perhaps it has already only you haven't heard about it."

"That's what I'm scared of," the sheriff conceded gloomily. "It ain't natural the way it is. Any minute I'm expecting some hellion to come busting in with bad news of some sort or other."

However, no messenger of ill omen arrived while Slade was in the saloon. After a while, thoroughly tired out by the long day of riding with very little rest the night before, he went to bed and slept late.

Shortly after midday found him in the saddle again, riding the trail that led to Tom Wardell's ranchhouse. This time he was not greeted with bullets but by something that doubtless had the potentialities for being just as dangerous or more so. Dolores was on the ranchhouse porch when he rode up to the steps. She called a cordial greeting and summoned a wrangler to care for Shadow.

"Come on in, Walt," she said. "I was just going to have something to eat. Dad and Tom aren't here. Sorry you missed them but perhaps you can put up with me."

"I'd be hard to satisfy if I couldn't," he instantly responded, falling in with her humor. "In fact, I think it was very considerate of them; now I can have you all to myself. But where are Tom and your father?"

Dolores proceeded to explain. "My Uncle John, Dad's brother, is coming up from the Nueces and bringing his herd with him, a very fine herd of improved stock, a big one. Dad finally persuaded him to come up here and settle. Dad and Tom have ridden to meet him."

"I see," Slade nodded. "Hope he'll like it up here, and I predict he will."

"I hope so, too," she said, "and I hope there'll be no more trouble here. I don't like the feud Dad has been carrying on with the people over to the east. I like to get along with my neighbors; we always did down in the Nueces country, and somehow I feel we will up here. I believe you caused Dad to do some hard thinking when you were here the other day. I think he's half inclined to agree with you that it is not the folks over to the east who are responsible for all the trouble. He doesn't set a guard on the trail any more."

"I'm glad to hear that," Slade told her. "I hope what I had to say had some effect on him."

"It certainly did," Dolores declared. "Really, it's remarkable the effect you have on people. Old Manuel, the cook, has been going around in a sort of ecstasy ever since you were here, Tom has developed a terrific case of hero worship and Sime Dobie chuckles every time your name is mentioned. It's astonishing."

Slade laughed and they walked to the dining room arm in arm.

They had a very pleasant dinner together and afterward sat in the living room and talked, chiefly about personal things. Finally, when the shadows were growing long, Slade glanced out the window and asked, "When do you expect the herd to roll in?"

"Oh, it won't get in today," she replied. "Uncle John had figured to run the cattle through Skull Canyon tonight after dark, but Dad and Tom rode down to tell him there's no sense in making the hard night drive. As I said, you have changed his notions about things. He's going to tell them to bed down the herd where they planned to stop this evening and wait for dark, several miles south of Skull Canyon, where I understand there's a belt of chaparral. Dad will ride back with them in the morning."

Slade stared at her, a pucker showing between his black brows. She quickly read his expression.

"Walt," she said, "you're worried about that herd, aren't you?"

As he hesitated, at a loss just how to frame a reply, she broke in before he could speak: "Listen, Walt, I was born and brought up on the rangeland. I understand and I'm familiar with all the hazards of the cattle business. Don't hesitate to tell me what is on your mind. I think I have a right to know. You are worried about it, aren't you?"

"Yes, Dolores, I am, and more so about your father and those with him. Funny things have been happening in this section of late; it would be foolish to disregard the fact. If I have persuaded him to believe the folks over to the east are not responsible for

the things that have happened and aren't out to make trouble for
him, he may be lulled into a sense of false security. I tell you what,
have my horse brought around. I'm going to ride down there and
tell him to be on his guard, just in case. Better to be safe than
sorry."

She hurried to obey and shortly Shadow was brought to the
foot of the steps.

"Don't worry, little lady, everything will be okay," he told her.

"I'm sure everything will be, with you handling the situation," she replied.

She walked down the steps with him. "But you'll be careful,
Walt?" she said as he swung into the saddle.

"Sure I will, and there's nothing for you to bother your pretty
head about," he told her cheerily and rode away.

But Slade was not nearly as much at ease as he led her to
believe. He had a disquieting premonition that something was
due to happen, a premonition not based on vagueness. The herd,
as she described it, would be a rare temptation to any outlaw
band. If Ellis Dawson was really operating in the section, and
Slade firmly believed he was, he would be loath to pass up such
an opportunity. He would very likely know of the coming of the
herd. The bedding place mentioned, as Slade remembered it from
his previous ride in the vicinity, offered favorable conditions for
a swift and deadly raid that would probably be successful unless
Wardell and the hands took precautions against just such an
eventuality. As Slade recalled the terrain, the probable bedding
place would be on the banks of a small stream with thick chaparral all around and no great distance away, ideal for a hole up.
And ideal for an outlaw who operated as Dawson always did,
absolutely without mercy. His system had always been to kill the
guardians of the cattle as his first move. He was coldly ruthless
and took no chances. The killing of the Circle K cattle guard and
the wounding of his companion, left for dead, and the attempted
drygulching of the sheriff's posse in Skull Canyon were examples

of how Dawson worked and there was no reason to believe that he would make an exception in his raid on Wardell's herd if he planned one. Slade felt that his only chance to save the Flying W owner and his companions was to get there and warn them before the rustlers made their move. He felt, however, that if a raid was premeditated it would hardly occur before the later hours of the night, when the camp had settled down to sleep.

"But we're not depending on that, feller," he told Shadow. "Sift sand, jughead!"

Shadow travelled at a fast pace that ate up the miles, but they had plenty of distance to cover and it was long past dark when they emerged from the south mouth of Skull Canyon. The night was bright with stars and twenty minutes later Slade could make out the darker clump ahead that was the widespread belt of chaparral. Five minutes more and he saw a glow above the brush tops that he knew must be from the fire that marked the site of the camp.

And now a new problem arose. Doubtless the Nueces cowboys, having listened to stories of the troubled section for which they were bound, were somewhat nervous and could be quick on the trigger, and a bit leary of anyone approaching the camp in the dark. It would be much safer to announce his arrival with loud shouts, but if the outlaws were somewhere in the vicinity, that would notify them also of his presence. Finally, when he figured he was within a couple of hundred yards of the camp, he dismounted and left Shadow in a little cleared space beside a trickle of water. With the greatest caution he stole forward through the growth and a few minutes later sighted the camp with the cowboys moving around the fire that had begun to die down, spreading their bed rolls and making preparations for sleep. A little farther on were the cattle, held in close herd on the banks of the brook. The fire was about a hundred yards from where he stood.

And now came the really ticklish part. He covered half the distance on hands and knees, moving with the silence of an

Indian, and then went down flat on his stomach, inching along through the tall grass, foot by slow foot, careful not to make the slightest sound or to set the grass heads waving too violently. It was nerve-wracking work and his forehead was damp when he at last reached a point only a few yards from where the Wardell brothers and their hands sat smoking beside the camp fire or finishing their nightly chores. He stood up and walked forward.

There was a storm of startled exclamations as the tall form of El Halcon strode into the circle of firelight. Men leaped to their feet and grabbed for their guns. Then old Tom recognized the unexpected visitor.

"Slade!" he exclaimed. "For the love of Pete! Where did you come from? Hold it, boys," he added quickly, "this is the young hellion I've been telling you about. Don't pay him no mind. That's a habit with him, just happening. John, shake hands with Walt Slade."

Slade shook hands with the other Wardell, a taller edition of old Tom but with twinkling, humorous eyes. Then he glanced around and shook his black head. If Ellis Dawson himself had arranged the camp it could not have been improved, from his viewpoint. It was perfect for drygulching. The fire had been built on a broad bench about fifteen feet above the lower ground where the stream ran. Directly across from it was a wall of tall and thick brush not more than twenty yards distant. Behind the camp the ground sloped upward gently to a second and broader bench sparsely grown with chaparral and some fifty feet above the first.

Slade wasted no time for idle conversation. In crisp, terse sentences he informed the Wardells of what he suspected might be in the wind.

"I may be wrong—hope I am," he concluded, "but it's best not to take chances."

"I wouldn't be a blamed bit surprised if you're right," old Tom declared explosively. "It would be right in line with what happened to me the first time I was up here. What shall we do, Slade?"

"First, scatter that fire a little so it'll die down faster, then roll your blankets to simulate sleeping men. I see you haven't posted a night guard yet."

"Don't need one," John Wardell explained. "Those tame critters won't stray and they hardly ever stampede. If something startles them they just bunch together and beller."

"I see," Slade said, "and that's all to the good. We don't have to worry about rigging up dummies to resemble riding night hawks."

Slade's orders were carried out efficienctly and with dispatch. Soon the bed rolls about the dying fire fairly simulated sleeping men wrapped in their blankets. Slade decided they should fool anyone surveying them from a distance.

"Now we'll sneak up to the bench above this one," he told the others. "We can't be seen up there but we can see anything that goes on down here."

The maneuver was executed cautiously and in silence. Soon John Wardell's hands, numbering fifteen, and the others, were crouched in the shadow of the slope, watching and waiting.

"Keep an eye on that brush clump across from the camp,' Slade directed. "I've a notion that if something is tried it will be from there."

A tedious and nerve-stretching hour passed, and the better part of another. It was just about midnight and Slade began to wonder if his hunch was a straight one. The wideloopers, if they really contemplated a raid, would hardly hold back much longer. They'd want several hours of darkness to get in the clear, especially if they intended to head north by way of Skull Canyon.

The hour completed and still nothing happened. A thin slice of late moon appeared in the east, casting a faint and elusive light over the prairie, strengthening the star glow but little. A very poor shooting light.

"I wish that brush was closer," Slade whispered to old Tom. "Mighty long range for sixguns, but there's nothing we can do about it."

Another ten minutes or so ticked off on the great clock wheeling westward in the sky. And then without the slightest preliminary warning, a roar of gunfire burst from the silent growth. The cowboys jumped and cursed under their breath, the cattle bawled, the blanket rolls by the almost dead fire jerked and twitched as bullets hammered them.

"The snake-blooded, murdering devils!" breathed old Tom.

The shooting ceased and for several moments there was no sound or movement, then drifting shadows appeared against the black background of the growth, horsemen starting to ride toward the milling herd.

"Let them get a little farther out," Slade whispered. "The range is too long."

Slade's heart was beating exultantly. It appeared his carefully planned ruse would bear delectable fruit.

And then the unpredictable happened. A nervous cowboy, shifting his weight from one foot to the other, stepped on a round stone that rolled under his boot. He floundered off-balance, failed to recover and fell, managing to let off his cocked gun so that the bullet passed within two inches of Slade's head. The report sounded like a thunderclap in the stillness. Instantly the moving shadows halted. Red flashes spurted from the darkness. Bullets buzzed like angry hornets.

"Let them have it!" Slade shouted as he jerked both guns and began firing as fast as he could pull trigger. But the shadowy horsemen whirled about and vanished before the cowhands could really get started shooting. There was a prodigious crashing in the brush, followed by the steady drumming of fast hoofs fading into the distance.

Slade swore a bitter oath and began ejecting the spent shells from his guns, but his habitual good humor quickly returned.

"Just one of those things that happen," he told the cursing Wardells. "I'm going to slide over to the brush and see if we had the luck to wing one."

"You're taking a chance," protested old Tom. "A wounded varmint of that stripe is dangerous as a busted-back rattler."

"I'll risk it," Slade replied, and glided down the slope, weaving and ducking, and across the open space to the brush. Nothing happened and a careful search of the growth discovered nothing. He came back to the others.

"No luck," he told them. "Well, anyhow, I've a notion we gave them a dang good scare and we won't be bothered with them any more tonight. I'll go get my horse. Blow up the fire and we'll heat some coffee and then everybody might as well go to bed. Fun's all over."

"Fun!" snorted old Tom. "When I think of what would have happened if we'd been in those bed rolls I get the jerks. Son, you've put all of us mighty heavy in your debt. Without you it would have happened. We won't forget it and if you ever need a hand in anything we'll be with you till the last brand's run. Want to have a little talk with you, tomorrow, too."

The coffee was drunk and the tired hands rolled up in their blankets and went to sleep. Slade sat by the fire for awhile, smoking and thinking. If he had had any doubt about it before, now he had not the slightest that Ellis Dawson was operating in the section. The current attempt had followed precisely the pattern of his depredations in the Red River country. And tonight, had it not been for an unfortunate mischance he might have bagged part or all of the murderous bunch. Oh, well, they couldn't keep getting the breaks forever! He joined the others in sleep.

CHAPTER TEN

NEXT DAY THE BIG HERD rolled slowly north through Skull Canyon. Slade rode in front, watchful and alert, but nothing untoward happened and nightfall found the cows safely bedded down on Tom Wardell's range.

That night was very much in the order of a celebration at the Flying W ranchhouse and it was late before Slade and old Tom had a chance to talk together. After everybody else had gone to bed, or so they thought, Wardell filled his black pipe with blacker tobacco, stretched out comfortably in an easy chair and regarded the Ranger through the blue mist of smoke.

"Well, son, I've been wanting to ask you something all day," he prefaced his remarks. "Do you aim to coil your twine in this section for a spell?"

"Possibly," Slade replied, "I don't know for how long."

"Well, if you do, I suppose you'll want to tie onto a job of riding for some outfit?"

"Well," Slade smiled, "I've always found that if a man doesn't work he doesn't eat."

"Exactly," chuckled old Tom, "which brings us to the nubbin of the ear. If you don't mind working with an outfit that's sort of on the outs with its neighbors, I'd take it mighty kind if you'd sign up with the Flying W."

"Perhaps the Flying W is not as much on the outs with its neighbors as you think, or at least won't be for long," Slade answered.

"I hope not," old Tom said soberly. "Down in the Nueces I always got along with everybody and I don't enjoy being on the prod against folks no matter what they do to me. Folks with Scotch blood have a reputation for being good haters, maybe we are, but I don't think we ever get much real pleasure out of hating."

"Hating is a sore that eats inward," Slade remarked.

"Never heard it put just that way, but it does sort of describe it pretty well," old Tom admitted. "But coming to what I was saying, I'd sure like to have you with us. Sime Dobie is my range boss and he's a good one, been with me for years, but like me he ain't young any more and can't get around like he used to. I need somebody to lend him a hand and keep my hellions in line. What do you say, son?"

Slade considered a moment. The proposition was not unattractive. It would provide him with a needed excuse for hanging around the section and he had a feeling that the Flying W would be the focus of developments.

"I wouldn't be surprised if I take you up on it, sir, and thanks for the offer," he replied. "We'll talk it over again in a day or two. Tomorrow I want to ride to town but I'll be back shortly and then we'll see."

"Okay, we'll let it go at that," said Wardell. "And now I'm going to bed. Sleeping out like last night ain't good for old bones. You sleep in the first room at the head of the stairs, on the right. I'm down at the far end of the hall and if you want something just let me know. Dobie sleeps right next to me. Stay up as long as you want to—the place is yours."

With a nod he lumbered off to bed. Slade sat alone for a while, smoking and thinking. Abruptly he realized he was not alone. Dolores had slipped silently down the stairs and stood beside him.

Slade rose to his feet quickly and bowed. Her big eyes regarded him seriously.

"You sit down and be comfortable again," she replied. "I just want to talk to you a little."

Slade sat down and she perched next to him.

"Now what do you want to talk to me about?" he asked.

Again she regarded him, very gravely. "Walt," she asked, "just who and what are you?"

"Well, I told you my name, and it's the one I got at the christening," he answered, "and if I go to work for your father I believe I'll be able to convince him that I'm a cowhand."

"Yes, she nodded, "doubtless you are, or were, but you haven't worked much at it for quite a while."

"How do you know?" he asked.

Her glance dropped to his hands. "You'll get rope blisters the first day," she replied.

He nodded. "What else do you see?" he wanted to know.

"Little callouses on your thumbs and first fingers," she said.

"Your eyes are good as well as beautiful," he admitted.

"Oh, we've had a few men with us who were always practicing the draw," she said. "Usually they didn't stay very long, and once or twice, after they'd ridden away, a sheriff or a Ranger dropped in to ask questions."

"And suppose a Ranger drops in and asks questions after I rode away. What will you tell him?" he asked laughingly. Her reply quickly sobered him.

"I'd tell him that if he really wanted to know where you were to go to the Ranger Post and find out," she said quietly.

Slade stared at her. "Just how did you arrive at your conclusion?" he asked.

"Oh, call it a woman's intuition, if you wish," she replied. "But I did talk to old Manuel, the cook, and he told me some things he knew concerning you. I just put two and two together and made five instead of four."

Slade shook his head. "You're too darn smart!" he grumbled.

CHAPTER ELEVEN

WHEN SLADE REACHED LUCAS the next day shortly after dusk, he headed for the sheriff's office. He found that official tired, dusty from long and hard riding and in a very bad temper.

"The Bar A, down to the south," he explained. "They lost about two hundred head last night. I've been riding through those infernal canyons all day. Didn't find a thing, of course."

"Anybody killed?" Slade asked quickly.

"Not this time, luckily," Sloan replied. "It was some tame stuff they'd driven onto good pasture around a waterhole. They aim to get a shipping herd together but they hadn't really started rounding up."

Slade nodded. Sloan regarded him fixedly for a minute. "Slade," he said, "do you still feel so sure those Nueces hellions ain't responsible for what's going on?"

"Well," Slade answered, "I've got something to tell you and then you can do a little thinking on it for yourself."

He related the attempt on John Wardell's herd and the abortive results. Sheriff Sloan rasped his unshaven chin with a forefinger and swore wearily. "Reckon they'd hardly be stealing from each other," he admitted grudgingly. Nothing but trouble and more trouble. I'm going loco."

Even then more trouble was on its way to the sheriff's office in the person of a big beefy individual with hard blue eyes and a shock of dark hair. He pulled up in front of the office, dropped the split reins to the ground, dismounted and entered.

"Why, hello, Val," the sheriff greeted him. "What's on your mind? I want you to meet Walt Slade. He's the feller I was telling you about, the one that kept us from getting dry-gulched in Skull Canyon. Slade, this is Val Russell who owns the Circle K."

Slade shook hands with Russell and liked his looks.

"What's on your mind, Val?" the sheriff asked. "Lose some more cows?"

"Nope, I haven't lost any more cows," Russell replied soberly. "I want to talk to you about my range boss, Phil Curry. You know Phil was always an arguing sort of a jigger and had a habit of taking views opposite to other folks."

"That's right," nodded the sheriff, apparently not noticing Russell's use of the past tense of the verb. Slade did, however. He leaned forward and listened intently to what the ranch owner had to say.

"Yes, Phil was that way," resumed Russell. "One of the things he argued against that most everybody else believed was that the cows stolen in this section weren't run north through Skull Canyon but right across the desert. He had a habit of prowling around out there trying to find out how it was done. Well, three days ago he ambled over in that direction. He didn't come back. We got bothered about him and rode over to try and find him. We got purty far out today and for a while I was figuring we'd most likely stay there. It's about as near hell out on those alkali sands as you're liable to find this side of the Big Jump. Reckon we never would have found him if it hadn't been we spotted the buzzards circling around. They led us to him, or what was left of him."

"Well, I'll be danged!" exclaimed the sheriff. "Poor old Phil! Heat got him, eh?"

"No, the heat didn't get him," Russell returned, his square face grim. "He'd been shot three times, in the back."

The sheriff's mouth dropped open. "You—you sure, Val?" he stuttered.

"Reckon my eyesight is still good as it ever was," replied the Circle K owner.

"But who the devil could have done it?" demanded Sloan. "I don't believe Curry had an enemy in the world."

"Well, somebody did it," said Russell. "I figure a bunch must have run him down. There hadn't been much wind for a day or two and there were hoof marks of a horse going mighty fast, but we didn't find his horse."

Walt Slade nodded his head. "You're right, sir," he said. "There were six of the hellions and they shot him out of the hull. I saw it."

His listeners stared at him with sagging jaws. "What—what the devil—" sputtered Sloan. "What you talking about, Slade?"

Briefly Slade related what he had seen mirrored in the sky as he sat his horse at the edge of the desert. His hearers, men familiar with the vagaries of the desert, nodded their understanding.

"Yes, you saw the devils do for poor Phil, all right," said Russell. "Nothing unusual about it except that you happened to be there at just the right time. Mirages do things like that, pick up things from the desert and show 'em up in the air. I rec'lect my grandpa telling about the time he saw a band of Indians riding through the sky. That was back in the days when the Indians raided from over in New Mexico and stole cows. Grandpa knew what he was seeing was the reflections of a bunch of Redskins riding across the desert. He figured about where they were most likely to strike and him and his hands were waiting for them when they showed up and gave the thievin' devils a larrupin' they didn't forget for a while. Killed five of them, I believe he said."

Slade looked very thoughtful. "And the Indians ran cows across into New Mexico?" he asked.

"That's what grandpa said," Russell replied. "Other old-timers said the same thing and I don't see how they could all have been mistaken."

"It could be done driving at night—two nights," Slade said, "but they'd have to hole up somewhere during the day, where there was water. Otherwise it couldn't be done."

"Maybe the Indians did know where there used to be water out there somewhere," said Russell, "but if they did they never told any white man about it. They were close mouthed about such things. Yes, maybe there was water back in those days, but there sure isn't any now. I've been across three times altogether and there's nothing but alkali sand and salt and rocks and hotter'n the hinges of hell. And if you get caught out there in a bad dust storm you've got a mighty good chance to cash in your chips. There isn't a drop of water to be found anywhere, and don't let anybody tell you there is."

"But you'll admit the Indians did run cows across," Slade persisted.

"According to the old-timers," Russell nodded. "Maybe there was a spring or something that finally got filled up with drifting sand."

"Possible but not probable," Slade replied. "Sand offers no insurmountable barrier to running water, and if water was rising to the surface it would continue to rise, no matter how much sand drifted. Would very likely end up forming a quicksand, but the moisture would still be there."

"Sounds good," conceded Russell, "but the fact remains there ain't. And now I'll tell you something else grandpa said. Quite a few times they tracked stolen cows a long ways out on the desert, but they always lost the trail. If there's just a little bit of wind, like there was today, the tracks fill right up. He said that a couple of times they tracked 'em nearly half way across and didn't see any water. And once after they lost the tracks they kept on going and way over to the other side, where there's less sand and where the wind didn't happen to blow much, they hit on the tracks again and followed them up into the hills, where of course they couldn't follow them far, not in those rocky canyons."

"Which meant," Slade said slowly, "that the Indians did get them across somehow, which they couldn't possibly have done if they didn't hole up for one day and have water for the cows."

Russell shrugged his big shoulders and threw out his hands.

"You talk about as good a case as poor Phil did," he admitted, "but there ain't no getting away from the fact that there ain't any water between this side of the desert and the other side."

"Or at least nobody has found it," Slade smiled.

"And anybody who goes looking for it is as short of brains as a terrapin is of feathers," Russell declared.

Slade chuckled, and did not argue the point. He was thinking of the "signboard" he saw in the old bison trail, which he did not mention to his companions.

The death of Phil Curry was further discussed, rather aimlessly, and no definite conclusion reached. Slade took little part in the conversation. He had his own theory as to why Curry was killed but did not care to voice it at the moment. He believed Curry had stumbled onto something the outlaws wanted kept secret. He had been spotted by them and killed.

The meeting broke up rather dismally after a futile session. Russell was depressed and gloomy because of the death of his range boss, the sheriff didn't know what to do about it and Walt Slade was in little better case. The killing of Phil Curry was another link in the chain he was trying to forge, and an important one, but there were still too darn many links missing. Convinced though he was that the outlaw Ellis Dawson was operating in the section, he still had not even a murky notion as to who Dawson was or where he was to be found. Bob Biggers fitted in pretty well with the vague description given of Dawson, but so did Val Russell, Carter Renshaw, or even old Tom Wardell, were his hair dyed black. Put a beard on the face of any of the men in question and he would conform after a fashion with what was known of Dawson's physical appearance.

Slade felt he had accomplished something. He had sowed seeds of doubt in the mind of old Tom Wardell, likewise in Sheriff Sloan's mind, and in Val Russell's. With the seeds growing just a bit, the danger of serious trouble between the two factions was lessened, although Slade knew well it would take very little to cause it to flare up again.

But this accomplishment, while laudible, was in the nature of a side issue. He had come to the Tucumcari Desert country with an express object in mind, the running down of Ellis Dawson and so far Dawson had been ordering things. Slade had frustrated him a couple of times, but that was all. Dawson was still on the loose with the potentialities of plenty of trouble. Slade knew he had his work cut for him and were it not for the ever present danger that more innocent persons would die because of Dawson's activities, he would have really enjoyed matching wits and guns with the elusive outlaw. As it was, he was in a constant state of apprehension Dawson might cut loose anywhere, and he was a killer, a type with which Slade was familiar, the weasel-type, courageous, restless, efficient, and like his animal prototype always hungry for blood.

A couple of drinks and a relaxing session of poker at the First Chance made everybody feel a bit better and ready for bed. Slade slept late and it was midafternoon when he headed for the Flying W. He had made up his mind to sign on with Tom Wardell.

Slade knew that Wardell had abandoned guarding the trail that led to his ranchhouse but he did not relax his vigilance. The initial attempt on his life in the stable had showed him that he was up against vicious killers with plenty of nerve and patience. His eyes constantly roved over growth and the slopes as he rode and missed nothing that went on around him. In consequence, he was surprised and exasperated when a slug whined high over his head and from a long ways up the right-hand slope came the crack of a rifle. A hit at such range would be nothing but a fluke. Nevertheless he took no chances and sent Shadow surging sideways into the growth. He dismounted and stole back on foot to peer through the fringe of brush flanking the trail.

It was Shadow's sudden explosive snort that saved him. He whirled at the sound, instinctively slewing sideways, and saw two men leaping toward him with drawn guns. He drew and shot with both hands, even as they pulled trigger.

A slug burned its way along his ribs, another ripped his sleeve. Ducking, weaving, he fired again and again. One of the attackers pitched forward to lie motionless, the other yelled with pain as a lucky bullet knocked his gun spinning and a portion of his hand with it. He cringed back from El Halcon's smoking Colts.

"Don't shoot, feller, don't shoot!" he cried hoarsely. "You've got me."

"Reckon I have," Slade agreed grimly. "Up! And turn around!"

The outlaw obeyed, jerking his hands, one dripping blood, high above his head and turning his back. Slade holstered one gun, moved forward cautiously and felt under his armpits, at the back of his neck and glanced down at his boot tops.

"Okay," he said and stepped back a couple of paces, "you can turn around now and lower your hands."

The fellow obeyed. His eyes were wide and staring, his mouth jerked. With his uninjured hand he mopped at the sweat that streamed down his face. With the wounded member he fumbled off his hat and wiped his forehead, holding the hat clumsily about shoulder high with his blood smeared fingers.

Just in time Slade saw the gleam of metal. He fired point blank even as the world seemed to explode in flame and roaring sound.

The outlaw fell back without a groan, drilled dead center. Slade spun around as if whirled by a giant hand and slumped to the ground. Shadow gazed inquiringly at his master and blew softly through his nose.

CHAPTER TWELVE

SLADE DID NOT WHOLLY LOSE CONSCIOUSNESS although bands of blackness weaved before his eyes, bell notes pealed in his ears and his entire body seemed paralyzed. But minutes passed before he was able to sit up and raise a shaking hand to his left temple where a few drops of blood oozed forth. The cut was trifling, but even a slight graze of a slug fired at close range packs a prodigious wallop. He regarded Shadow owlishly, for his mind was still a bit foggy.

"Thanks, feller," he said thickly. "Reckon you saved my bacon with that snort. Well, I thought I knew about all there was to know about gun totin', but that was a new one. The hellion had a derringer cached in his hat! Nervy devil, taking a chance with me holding my gun on him. And he came darned close to getting away with it. An inch to the right and I'd be coyote fodder, too."

He got to his feet, groggily, shaking his head to free it of the last lingering cobwebs and started to examine the bodies of the two dead men. He had barely noted that they were hard looking specimens, when he abruptly remembered something that sent him diving for the shelter of a thick bush. Where the devil was the unseen rifleman who had baited the trap from a safe distance?

Minute after minute Slade crouched motionless, not daring to make a sound that might reveal his presence were the drygulcher nearby and stalking him. He had but a vague notion of how long he had lain dazed. The fellow could have had time to work his way down through the brush to see how his companions had made out. For all Slade knew he might even now be hiding behind the nearest tree trunk. Finally, with the utmost care, he groped about until his fingers encountered a small boulder half buried under fallen leaves. He worked it free from its bed and tossed it underhand. It rustled through the growth, making a creditable imitation of somebody moving stealthily about.

Nothing happened. Birds continued to chirp. A little animal pattered past his hiding place on tiny paws. The shadows were curdling under the bushes. Slade itched to get a closer look at the two dead outlaws, who in the quick glance he gave them had a vaguely familiar look; but he feared to take the risk.

Somewhere not far off a horse neighed impatiently. Was it one of those that must have been ridden by the slain pair, or did it belong to the third member of the unsavory trio? Slade didn't know and there was no way to find out. He eased himself into a little less strained position and schooled himself to patience. There was nothing to do but wait for darkness. Then he would be on an even footing with the third drygulcher were he still hanging around.

Finally with the gloom thick under the growth he decided to take a chance. He straightened up, waited a minute and then glided to where Shadow stood, dimly seen in the deepening dusk. Again he waited, peering and listening, before swinging into the saddle.

"Okay, feller, if we can't make it now we never can," he muttered and sent the black charging for the trail. He reached it without anything happening and turned Shadow's head north. He wasn't feeling any too good and resolved to make for the Flying W without delay. He'd ride down in the morning and give the bodies a once-over. He was fairly well assured that the third drygulcher was not around but preferred not to play his luck too strong.

As he rode he shook his head in silent admiration of the ingenuity shown by the rascals he was up against. He had encountered shoulder holsters, sleeve holsters, waistband holsters and boot-top holsters; but a hat holster was a new wrinkle. The hellions sure had novel notions.

And the trap laid for him had been most cleverly conceived. Apparently not caring to take a chance with the rider who had proven his alertness they had worked out a scheme that involved a minimum of danger to themselves. With his attention distracted by the drygulcher far up the slope, the other two had lain in wait, ready to take advantage of the opportunity provided by his concentration on the unseen rifleman. And they had very nearly gotten away with it. Only the watchfulness of his horse and his constant attention to any unusual action on the part of the intelligent animal had saved him.

There was another angle that puzzled Slade a little. He felt that the two outlaws had wanted to take him prisoner if possible. Because of which they had held their fire just an instant too long, with disastrous results so far as they were concerned. Well, it had all worked out a lot better than he thought it would when the whirlwind action began. But his respect for the man against whom he was opposed had heightened. Walt Slade was unusually fast with a gun and correspondingly accurate, but he knew there were plenty of men on the other side of the corral fence who were just as fast and just as accurate. Quicker thinking had many times tipped the balance in his favor, but he was beginning to wonder if he held any such advantage over Ellis Dawson. He rode on feeling a bit better but with his head still ringing from the effects of the slug that slammed his skull and with an unpleasant burning where the other bullet had ripped along his ribs.

There was considerable of a tumult when Slade entered the Flying W living room where Dolores and old Tom sat reading.

"What the devil happened to you?" demanded the ranchowner. "You look all beat up and there's blood on your face."

"Just a little run-in," Slade told him cheerfully. "Nothing to bother with."

"There's a bullet hole in your shirt!" exclaimed Dolores.

"Just a scratch," Slade deprecated the injury.

"Take it off!" she ordered. "Don't argue with me, take it off, I say. I want to see about that 'scratch'."

Slade obeyed, baring his sinewy back and shoulders. Dolores exclaimed over the ragged furrow an inch or two below his heart and went to work on the wound with antiseptic salve, a bandage and court plaster.

Old Tom gazed at Slade admiringly. "Golly, what a pair of arms you got, son!" he marveled. "Bet they could crack ribs easy if you really put the pressure on."

After the wound was dressed to Dolores' satisfaction and Slade had donned his shirt, old Tom said, "Now we'll go and eat and you can tell us what happened."

As he ate, Slade told them. Dolores looked decidedly worried. Old Tom swore explosively.

"The hellions are out to get you, son," he declared. "You tangled their twine for them a couple of times and they're out to even up the score."

"Looks sort of that way, but they haven't had much luck so far," Slade returned composedly. "Tomorrow morning I'll ride down and look over the scalps."

"But not alone," Wardell said in a voice that forbade argument. "I'll go with you and we'll take along three or four of the boys; then if the mangy toads come looking for trouble they'll get it till it runs out of their ears. I got a prime hankering to swap lead with the devils and sure hope I get a chance to. My eyes may not be just what they used to be but I'm still pretty good with my old Smith. Now we'll have a smoke and then you'd better get to bed and give that head a rest. Reckon it was a forty-one the sidewinder had cached in his hat and those short guns pack a hefty wallop at close range."

Slade did go to bed shortly afterward. After a good night's rest, aside from a bit of stiffness he was back to normal. With

Wardell, Sime Dobie and three more Flying W hands he rode back to where he had the run-in with the owlhoots.

"Guess this is about it," he announced as he pulled Shadow to a halt. "Yes, there's the broken brush where we went into it. The bodies should be just beyond that bristle."

They should have been, but they weren't. There was not a sign of the two dead men. Slade quartered the ground for a considerable distance and found nothing. Coming back to the spot where he holed up after the shooting, he picked up the spent shells he had ejected from his guns.

"Proves that right here was where it happened," he observed. "Wanted to be sure I wasn't making a mistake as to the exact locality. I wasn't."

"But what does it mean?" demanded old Tom.

"It means, I'd say, that somebody wasn't overly anxious to have those bodies put on display in Lucas," Slade replied quietly.

"Afraid they'd be recognized, eh?" said Wardell.

"Not an illogical assumption," Slade admitted, "or at least that they might be recognized as having been seen associating with somebody," he qualified.

"Sounds like you're sort of admitting that maybe the bunch over to the east is mixed up in the deal," observed Wardell.

"I'm not generalizing," Slade replied, "but it is not beyond the realm of possibility that somebody over to the east is mixed up in it, just as it is not impossible that somebody up to the north is."

"I'll vouch for my neighbors," growled Wardell.

"And for every hand who works for them?" Slade asked pointedly.

Old Tom tugged his mustache and grudgingly admitted that might be covering a bit too much territory.

"Exactly," Slade said. "More than one honest rancher has all of a sudden awakened to the fact that some off-color gents have been wearing his brand. It's often surprising in what barrel you can find a rotten apple if you look close enough."

"And one rotten apple usually gathers some more around it before long," Wardell nodded.

"States the case precisely," Slade agreed. "The great trouble right now is that we don't know which barrel to examine. Might as well be getting back to the spread. I'd figured on a talk with the sheriff, but there isn't much sense in that the way things stand. No use confessing to a couple of killings when you can't produce any remains to back it up."

Old Tom chuckled and 'lowed it made sense. They turned their horses and rode back to the Flying W, arriving at the ranchhouse shortly before noon.

"Well, son," said old Tom as they headed for the dining room and a bite to eat, "going to sign on with me?"

"Reckon I could do worse," Slade replied, smiling at Dolores, who blushed a little and smiled back.

"Fine!" applauded Wardell. "After dinner we'll saddle up and ride around a bit so you can give things a once-over."

About an hour later they got the rigs on their horses and started out, heading north by east.

"All open range here," explained Wardell. "Us folks from the Nueces ain't got no use for wire."

"Perhaps not, but you'll have to come to it sooner or later," Slade predicted. "You'll learn that you can't compete with spreads that have adopted wire. Fenced range obliviates the tedious and costly process of the round-up, the cows are easier to work on fenced range, you can get a shipping herd ready much faster and you're better protected against stealing. They've already learned the lesson in the upper Panhandle. Miles of wire there and more being strung all the time."

"I don't like these darned newfangled notions," grumbled old Tom.

"I understand how you feel," Slade replied, "but this system of ours does not permit of standing still. We either have to walk ahead or slide back. And that applies especially to cattleland. The day of the open range is drawing to a close."

"I'm afraid maybe you're right," Wardell admitted morosely. "Oh, well, I'm getting a bit too old to bother my head much about it. I'll let you youngsters battle it out."

They rode steadily for several hours and Slade got a good notion of what was needed to get the most from the big spread. They passed through a grove, for there was more than the usual number of trees in this particular locality, and Slade suddenly uttered an exclamation of pleasure.

"Somebody has got a good eye for color," he observed.

His gaze was resting on a small but tightly built ranch-house set on a low rise and close to a broad trail running north and south. The walls were a glittering white, the window frames and the shutters were green, the roof a bright red. A yellow striping encircled the building, passing under the window ledges. The effect, Slade thought, was original and very pleasing.

"Purty, ain't it?" chuckled old Tom. "That's Carter Renshaw's *casa*. We're on his land right now. It was just an old shack when he bought it from Berne Holt who wanted to move east, on the easy payment plan—some down and then regular installments as the spread pays off. He fixed it up and painted it and made a darn good-looking house of it. He's a smart cowman. Not a very big spread and he don't use many hands, but he's got good stock and handles it well. What say we ride over and visit with him if he's home? He 'pears to be a pretty nice sort."

"Could do worse, I reckon," Slade agreed.

In answer to Wardell's shout, Carter Renshaw himself appeared in the doorway.

"Light off and cool your saddles," he called hospitably. "How are you, Mr. Wandell?"

"Fine as frog's hair," replied old Tom. "I want you to know Walt Slade, who's signed up to help me run things. Walt, this is Carter Renshaw, you may have heard of him."

"I saw Mr. Renshaw in town the other night," Slade acknowledged as they shook hands. Renshaw's grip was powerful and firm.

"I believe I saw you, too, Mr. Slade, talking with our good sheriff," said Renshaw. "Glad you've decided to stay with us a while. But you can expect some of the old-timers to look at you sort of sideways. They do at me, just because I'm a newcomer here. They don't take kindly to invasions."

"Danged old stick-in-the-muds!" growled Wardell.

"Guess the old-timer down in the Nueces country are somewhat different," Slade observed seriously.

Old Tom tried to frown but ended up grinning. "Oh, we got 'em down there, too," he admitted. "Reckon you'll find them everywhere. Some of 'em are mighty set in their ways."

"Yes, don't take to new-fangled notions," Slade remarked.

"That has all the earmarks of a nice little dig in the ribs with a pitchfork," said Wardell, "but we'll let it pass. You young squirts think you know it all."

"Come in, come in," said Renshaw. "Take a load off your feet."

He led the way to the living room of the ranchhouse, which was comfortably furnished. Slade was struck by the harmonious color scheme.

Renshaw proved to be a charming host. He made coffee and unearthed a plate of very tasty cakes, conversing smoothly and pleasantly the while. He was undoubtedly a man of some culture, Slade decided.

His eyes interested the Ranger. They were black as an Indian's and, as is sometimes the case with the Comanches and Apaches, with a peculiar opaqueness to them, like to the eyes of the bird of prey. He wondered if Renshaw had some Indian blood.

However, if he did, his other features did not show it. His nose was well formed and straight, with not hint of the aquiline, his cheek bones low and his face rather broad across the cheek bones. His lips were thin and straight. In build he was also unlike the lank Plains Indians, being rather on the massive side. Slade judged him to be somewhere around forty, perhaps a little less.

After spending a pleasant hour with the Bradded R owner they headed for the Flying W. On a rise Slade turned to look back at the ranchhouse, his eyes thoughtful.

"Red, yellow and green on a white background," he muttered under his breath. "Red, yellow and green! Sort of a funny coincidence."

CHAPTER THIRTEEN

SEVERAL BUSY BUT UNEVENTFUL days followed. Tom Wardell had decided to get a shipping herd together. Sime Dobie was pretty well out of commission from an attack of sciatica, and the chore of getting the shipping herd together fell largely to Slade. And very shortly old Tom was congratulating himself loudly on the tophand he had hired in the nick of time to take over Dobie's work. He quickly decided that Walt Slade knew more about the cattle business than all the rest of them put together. In addition, he had the knack of handling men. The Flying W hands were a turbulent bunch, especially the younger element, but they quickly learned that this tall, leveleyed stranger was range boss.

This was proven conclusively at Plaino, the cowtown fifteen miles to the northeast where the Nueces cattlemen did their buying. Slade and three of the hands had ridden to Plaino to purchase needed supplies, taking along a light wagon. It was late when they reached the town and it was decided to stay over night. Slade turned the boys loose for a few hours of relaxation in the saloons and dance halls, the most popular of which with the Nueces men was the Lone Ace, a combination saloon, restaurant and dance hall.

One of the three hands was big Curly Mason, a two-fisted, hulking cowboy with bristling red hair who was the acknowledged leader of the younger faction. Mason was a skilled and excellent worker, but inclined to be belligerent, and with a few snorts of redeye under his belt was liable to get quarrelsome and ugly. He always did what Slade told him to do, but El Halcon sensed a certain resentment on the part of the big redhead. It was common knowledge that Mason expected to succeed Sime Dobie as range boss when the latter retired from active range work and it didn't set well with him when Slade was appointed to what amounted to foreman over the outfit.

About midnight Slade decided it was time to call a halt to the festivities. "We'll make this the last one," he said. "Time to go to bed. We've got work to do tomorrow and hangovers don't make for good performance."

Two of the hands nodded compliance, but Curly Mason grumbled. "The night's just begun," he protested.

"Maybe for some folks who haven't anything to do, but it's finished for us," Slade replied.

Mason bristled. "Tarnation! I ain't used to taking orders from somebody when I ain't in the hull," he growled.

"Get used to it and stay healthy," Slade told him.

Mason glared. "Like the devil I will, you dang range tramp!" he bawled.

Slade's reaction to the affront was instant and explosive. His left hand lashed out and took Mason squarely across the mouth, hard. Mason reeled back, blood spurting from his cut lips. He gave a yell of fury and charged, head down, huge fists flailing.

Slade weaved sideways and whipped an overhand right to Mason's jaw. The big puncher's feet left the floor, his long body sailed through the air and hit the floor with a crash that set the hanging lamps to dancing. He came off the floor like a rubber ball and rushed again.

Slade hit him, left and right, rocking him back on his heels, but Mason shook his head and came on again, throwing punches with both hands.

Walt Slade, alert and watchful, instantly realized that Mason knew how to use his hands and could hit like the kick of a mule. A punch got past his guard and caught him squarely on the cheek bone with stunning force. Another smashed into his ribs and sent him reeling back against the bar. He slashed Mason with a vicious left hook but did not stop him. They closed, hammering each other with lefts and rights. Slade jolted the cowboy's body with short wicked punches that brought grunts from him. A pile driver to his own wind left him gasping for breath. He broke from the deadly clinch and shot a right-cross to Mason's jaw, rocking him back on his heels once more. Then a hard drive to his own jaw sent red flashes storming before his eyes and filled his mouth with a taste of sulphur. Mason let out a whoop and dived forward to follow up his advantage.

With paralyzing suddenness the end came. Slade went sideways along the bar, blocked the lethal blow aimed at his chin and his right hand came up from somewhere in the neighborhood of his knee with all his two hundred pounds of muscular weight behind it. His slim, steely fist hit Mason's jaw with a smack like a butcher's cleaver on a side of meat.

Mason whirled in his tracks, staggered, and crashed to the floor with his bloody face buried in the sawdust. He did not rise.

Slade stepped back warily, dashing the blood from his eyes, his gaze fixed on the other two cowboys whom he knew to be personal friends of Curly Mason.

But the two punchers made no hostile move. They stood stiffly, staring with unbelief at the tall Ranger. One shook his head dazedly, as if to free his brain of cobwebs.

"If I hadn't seen it I wouldn't believe it, ain't sure about it even if I did see it!" he said in mumbling tones. "Curly Mason knocked cold!"

He shook his head again and continued to stare at Slade. "Feller," he said, "you just did what ain't never been done before. I've seen Curly Mason fight for fifteen years and I ain't never seen him knocked off his feet before. A great big jigger knocked him sideways once before Curly finished him, but that's the best anybody was ever able to do, before tonight. I take off my hat to you!"

Walt Slade's teeth flashed white in his bronzed face and his gray eyes were all dancing lights of laughter. "I reckon maybe he slipped on the wet floor," he said, apropos of the fallen Mason who was moving and muttering with returning consciousness.

"Yeah," the cowboy agreed dryly, "yeah, he slipped all right! I hope I don't ever slip that way. It's too dang hard on the teeth!"

Slade chuckled and wiped the blood from his own lips. He crossed lithely to where Mason lay, knelt beside him and turned him over on his back. Mason shook his head, opened his blue eyes and stared up at the man who had whipped him. Then he leaped to his feet and stood before Slade, who had also straightened up. His split lips spread in a wide grin.

"I'm used to it," he said briefly and turned to his companions. "Let's go, boys," he told them. "The boss says it's time to hit the hay."

An amusing aftermath to the rukus, which Slade heard about later, occurred the day before the shipping herd was to take the trail.

"Curly and me had picked up that stuff in Plaino you wanted for the chuck wagon and stopped at the Lone Ace for a drink before heading back to the spread," a cowboy who was present told old Tom. "Somehow or other the talk got onto Walt Slade. A big mean looking feller packing two guns said he saw him that other night we were up there and didn't like his looks. 'Lowed he'd bear a mite of watchin'. Well, Curly sort of sighed, picked up a bottle and busted it over the feller's head. Feller didn't come to for half an hour and when he did he 'lowed he'd sort of reconsidered and that Slade was just about the finest jigger he ever laid eyes on. 'Pears it ain't exactly good business to say anything against Slade when Curly's around."

"Curly always 'lowed he could love a man who could lick him," chuckled old Tom.

CHAPTER FOURTEEN

THE SHIPPING HERD got underway on schedule. It was a big one, nearly fifteen hundred head, and worth plenty. Wardell needed the money to finish paying for his land and to lend some to his brother.

"I'm depending on you to get her through," he told Slade. "Reckon I ain't got anything to worry about, though."

The drive was conducted in the time-honored fashion of the rangeland. Nobody rode immediately in front of the herd, although usually the trail boss rode far ahead to hunt out water, grass and suitable bedding ground. In this instance, with the bedding-down spot chosen in advance, it was not necessary for Slade to forge ahead and survey the locality. At times, however, he would scout ahead a bit to become familiar with the ground over which the herd would pass and give any dubious terrain a careful once-over.

The objective of the drive was a little way station something more than thirty miles to the northeast where there were sidings and loading pens for the convenience of the cattlemen of the section. The tiny settlement consisted only of a little cubbyhole office for the telegraph operator and agent and a few shacks occupied by railroad workers. Slade hoped to complete the chore of driving and loading in two days.

The first day out the herd rolled steadily northward without incident. The weather was excellent and the going good. That night camp was made in an open space where there was good grass and a little stream. Double night guards were set although there was little chance that anybody could even get near the herd without being spotted. But on the afternoon of the second day Slade noted something of interest. Finally he rode up beside Curly Mason who was riding point.

"Don't make it obvious but keep an eye on the slope to the right about a thousand yards up," he told the cowboy. "See if you can't spot a jigger up there pacing his horse parallel to our course."

Muttering profanity under his breath, Mason did so. After several minutes passed he suddenly uttered an exclamation.

"By gosh, there is somebody up there!" he said. "I spotted him as he passed that limestone outcrop. What the devil!"

"I don't know," Slade admitted, "but he's been there ever since we entered this range of hills. Twice I caught a shine from his bridle irons or gun handle, then I got a glimpse of him where the brush was a bit thin. Spotted him two or three more times. It doesn't seem to make sense that anybody would make a try for a herd guarded as this one is, but he's sure keeping a close watch on us for some reason or other. Is there any place ahead where a try might be made?"

"Not a place," declared Mason. "All like this till we get through the hills, which ain't far, and then it's open prairie all the way to the railroad. Up past these hills is the real beginning of the Plains. The other side of the railroad you'll hardly ever see a tree between here and Amarillo."

Slade shook his head. "No, it doesn't make sense," he repeated, "but to all appearances somebody is keeping tabs on our progress for some reason or other, and you can bet that it's not a good one. Somebody has something in mind. I sure wish I knew what the devil it could be."

"I give up," conceded Mason. "As you say, it sure don't make sense."

Another hour and they reached the open prairie and the mysterious horseman was seen no more, but Slade didn't forget him and kept cudgeling his brains for an explanation of his seemingly senseless behavior.

More than an hour before sunset they reached the railroad. Stock cars had been arranged for in advance and full dark had not yet fallen when the last cow was behind a closed door. Slade breathed a sigh of relief. No matter what might happen, at least the herd was now the railroad's responsibility and he and Tom Wardell could rest easy on that score.

But nevertheless Slade felt that as a Texas Ranger he was not finished with the business. Something was in the wind. What it could be he hadn't at the moment the slightest notion but the premonition persisted that some sort of skullduggery was in the making.

After the loading was finished he went to confer with the telegraph operator and learned that a locomotive and a caboose would arrive from the west at about ten o'clock and pick up the train. He digested this bit of information for a few minutes, then abruptly asked a question. "Where's the first stop they make?"

"About five miles to the east where there's a water tank," the agent replied. "They take on water there. What we've got here is okay for the cows but it's a bit alkaline and foams in the boiler."

"And that would mean water working through the throttle and into the steam chests and the cylinders," Slade observed. "Might knock out a cylinder head."

The agent regarded him curiously. "You talk like you've been around railroads a bit, cowboy," he remarked.

"Some," Slade admitted absently, for his thoughts were else-where. He was silent and distraught while the evening meal was prepared and eaten. Then for some time he sat smoking and gaz-ing eastward across the star burned prairie. Far in the distance he could see some groves and belts of thickets, and it appeared that an arm of the hills through which they had passed late in the afternoon reached out some distance to the north from the parent body. By way of which it would have been possible for the rimrock rider that so intrigued him to proceed unseen almost to the railroad right-of-way. Abruptly he pinched out his cigarette and called to Curly Mason.

"Curly," he said when the big cowboy lumbered up, "how'd you like a little excitement?"

"Fine!" Mason instantly responded; "it's been a blamed dull trip. What's on your mind, Boss?"

"I've a notion," Slade replied, "that if we take a little ride over east we may find some."

"Say, will you please tell me what the devil you mean?" pleaded the bewildered puncher.

"I mean," Slade said, "that I've got a mighty strong hunch that some hellions are going to make a try for those cows when the engine stops to take on water at the tank to the east of here. That fellow we spotted up in the hills this afternoon wasn't riding up there just for fun. He was keeping tabs on us so, I figure, he could report to somebody else when we'd be due here. Once they figured that out, having doubtless learned when the pick-up engine would come along and knowing it would stop at the tank for water, they'd be all set for a raid. I recall something similar that happened on the Southern Pacific just west of Sanderson at the edge of the Big Bend country. The devils got away with it, too. Unloaded nearly a thousand prime beef critters and ran them south to Mexico before anybody figured out what had happened. Up here would be even easier. Trains run infrequently on this line and nothing could come from farther east till the cattle train clears. They'd have a head start to New Mexico before word got east to a sheriff's office."

Mason swore explosively. "Feller, danged if I don't believe you've hit on something," he declared. "Let's get the devils!"

"Do you think some of the boys would care to go along?" Slade asked seriously.

Big Curly chuckled, fully appreciating the joke. "Well," he drawled, "I know eleven that will. Don't reckon we've got time to run down to the home spread and get the rest of the outfit we left down there. Guess Manuel, the cook, had better stay here, though, to keep an eye on the wagon and the remuda. When do we start?"

"Right away," Slade decided. "By so doing I believe we'll have a chance to get there first. If they get there first, hole up and spot us coming we'll very likely meet a lively reception. I'm not concealing the fact that this chore packs considerable danger. It's a bad bunch and will stop at nothing. So it's up to you fellows to do whatever you think best."

"I'll tell the boys and we'll get ready," Mason answered.

Ten minutes later the outfit was riding swiftly across the prairie, heading for the dotting of groves and the long bristle of chaparral growth that flanked the right-of-way on the south. They reached the rather dubious shelter of the first grove without incident. From there Slade took a chance on leading his troop across a wide stretch of open ground to the chaparral which also was broken by clumps of trees. In the welcome shadow they drifted along at an easy pace.

The night was brilliant with stars and a faint but strengthening glow in the east told of the late moon that would appear before long. They were still more than a mile from their destination when the silver curve peeped over the horizon. A few moments later, from the crest of a low swell of ground, they saw the spider-legged bulk of the big water tank outlined against the paling stars.

Slade called a halt in a grove a bit to the south of the eastward flowing straggle of chaparral.

"Can't risk taking the horses any farther," he told his companions. "We'll tie them here under the trees and slip across to the brush on foot. If we're not spotted before we get there we should be okay."

"And if we are, it won't matter much to some of us," Curly Mason predicted grimly.

It was ticklish work, crossing the open stretch in the strengthening light. The crunch of a boot on a dry patch of grass, the little sputter of an overturned pebble and even the faint rustling of the waist-high grass as they passed through it sounded frighteningly loud in the vast stillness. Although the night was not warm, everybody was sweating a bit by the time they reached the shadow of the growth without hearing, or feeling, the lethal whine of lead and the nerve-shattering crackle of gunfire.

At the edge of the chaparral, the belt of which was perhaps a hundred yards wide, a consultation was held.

"Now we've got to split up," Slade said. "Curly, you and half the boys will slide along a little farther and then hole up close to the tracks. The rest of us will go on to the water tank. That train will be more than a half-mile long and we've got to take care of both ends of it. If the hellions do plan a raid they'll hit the engine and the caboose at the same time. Curly, if things really start you must move fast. If it's the bunch I think it is they won't hesitate to murder the trainmen, may do so right at the beginning so there'll be no witnesses left and nobody to take the alarm back to the telegraph station. I wouldn't put it past them. So when you see them make a run for the caboose, hit them hard. Don't let them get the jump on you in any way or it's liable to be curtains for some or all of you. I've a notion you'll have the edge on them in numbers or be close to even, anyhow, and the element of surprise should work in your favor. But, I repeat, don't let them surprise you. Keep under cover till you're sure what's going on, and watch out for some of them hanging back and catching you between a cross-fire. Okay? All right, then, straight ahead for a couple of hundred yards and then slide into the growth and work your way to the last straggle this side of the tracks. Let's go!"

A little later Slade watched Mason and his hands slip noiselessly into the brush and vanish. He led his own group on until they were almost opposite the shadowy loom of the water tank. Then they in turn diagonalled through the thick bristle until they were almost to the right-of-way and some twenty paces to the west.

"I figure they'll come from the southeast," he explained in whispers to his men. "That's their logical route, up through that arm of the hills. We won't be able to see them arrive and we'll be lucky if we hear them. Okay, no more talking above a whisper and the less of that the better."

CHAPTER FIFTEEN

THERE FOLLOWED A LONG AND TRYING WAIT, the most disagreeable part of a fight in which one grows nervous and begins to reflect earnestly on one's sins. Even Slade, who had had considerable experience with such affairs, was not as comfortable as he might have been and the punchers were decidedly jumpy.

In fact Slade was not altogether easy in his mind as to the outcome, especially the action that would center around the distant caboose. The outlaws were desperate men and doubtless expert in the use of hardware whereas, contrary to popular opinion, Slade knew that hard working cowboys who had little time for the extensive practice of marksmanship were generally anything but good shots. However he understood that Mason knew how to handle a gun and the same went for one or two of his men. Well, all he could do was hope for the best.

Tediously the minutes passed, became an hour and the best part of a second. The moon was well up in the sky now and the twin ribbons of the railroad gleamed and glittered frostily. The growth was utterly silent and devoid of motion with not even a breath of wind to stir the leaves and if there was any animal life present it apparently slept the sleep of the just. Then suddenly one of the punchers hissed a whisper.

"Say, didn't I hear a train whistle?"

"You did," Slade whispered back, "and if you listen close you'll hear something else. Somebody's riding through the brush a couple of hundred yards to the east. Now they've stopped. Hear that saddle pop as somebody unforked? Quiet, now, and set. Here comes the train and the ball's about ready to open. We've played a straight hunch."

Slade trained his ears to catch any further movement in the growth in the hope of estimating just how many rustlers they would be up against. He felt that they could hardly hope that in numbers the odds would be much in their favor if at all. He figured there would be at least a dozen of the wide-loopers. Fewer would be unable to handle the chore of unloading the herd and getting it moving in anything like a reasonable length of time. The only advantage he and his men enjoyed, so far as he could see, rested on the element of surprise that was in their favor.

The rails were humming now. The whistle note sounded again, much nearer, and they could hear the labored thunder of the exhaust as the big locomotive pitted its might against the pull of the long train of loaded cars. Another moment and the headlight beam flickered the rails and outlined the water tank. Abruptly the crackle of the exhaust shut off and the rumble of the wheels sounded loud. Came a screech of brake shoes grinding against the tires, the clatter of the air pumps and the hiss of escaping steam. The huge bulk of the engine appeared. The bellowing of the cattle sounded. Another screech of brakes and the train ground to a stop, the panting engine opposite the water tank.

"Get set!" Slade whispered to his men. "Don't let them make it into the engine cab."

But despite Slade's care, tragedy struck. There was the crack of a shot and a cry of pain from the cab. The engineer, who had been leaning out the window, slumped back and disappeared. From the growth dashed shadowy figures, six or seven of them, and ran toward the locomotive.

"Let them have it!" Slade shouted, shooting with both hands.

The triumphant yelps of the outlaws changed to yells of surprise and alarm. One pitched forward on his face, a second fell sideways, thrashing and kicking. The others whirled about and returned the fire. Bullets zipped through the growth, showering down leaves and twigs. A cowboy cursed viciously, another uttered a gasping groan. Slade dashed forward, his guns blazing. A third outlaw went down. His companions fled for the shelter of the growth. A fourth dropped dead before they reached it. There was a prodigious crashing and a pounding of fast hoofs. The cowboys emptied their guns into the chaparral as the beat of hoofs faded into the distance.

"Hold it!" Slade shouted. "Listen!"

From the rear of the train came a stutter of shots followed by a crackling volley and then an evenly spaced banging.

"What the devil?" barked a puncher as he shoved fresh cartridges into the cylinder of his Colt.

"Sounds like some of them back there made it to their horses and the boys are throwing lead after them," Slade deduced. "Make sure of those devils on the ground while I see about the engineer."

The fireman, a guttering torch in his hand, dropped from the engine cab. His eyes were wild and staring and he was shaking as if with ague.

"Mahoney's up there," he gasped. "I think he's killed."

Slade quickly climbed into the cab and found the engineer, a scrawny, elderly man with a leathery face, slumped on the floor against his seatbox. He was clutching an arm with reddened fingers and swearing profusely.

"Let's have a look," Slade told him. He deftly cut away the sleeve of the jumper and shirt and examined the wound.

"Just a clean hole through the fleshy part," he told the hogger. "I'll tie it up and you'll be okay till you see a doctor. Isn't bleeding much and no bones broken."

The old man was filled with surly courage. "Go to it," he said. "Did you get any of the sidewinders?"

"Four up here, I think, and maybe some more back at the rear end," Slade told him as he went to work on the injured member.

"Good!" growled the engineer. "I feel better already. Give me a cigarette, will you?"

Slade twisted the bandage, a strip torn from his shirt, into place and rolled a cigarette. He placed it between the engineer's lips and touched a match to it. The oldster puffed vigorously between curses.

"What the devil were they after, the cows?" he asked.

"Reckon that was the general notion," Slade replied. "Take it easy now till I see if any of my boys need attention. I think one or two of them got nicked."

His apprehension on that score was quickly relieved, however. One puncher had a rip in the top of his shoulder, another had suffered a gashed cheek. They were attending to their own injuries and declined assistance.

"Cut myself worse shaving, many a time," declared the man with the gouged cheek.

The dead outlaws had been hauled together and the other hands were examining them by the aid of the fireman's torch. As Slade joined them, Curly Mason came into view, breathing hard and limping in his high-heeled boots, for he had run the whole length of the train.

"How is it up here?" he panted. "We got three. The rest made it to their horses and hightailed. "Just two, I think. No, nobody got hurt except for a couple of nicks. We caught 'em plumb off balance and they shot like kindergarten kids. Say, these hellions have a familiar look to 'em. I'd swear I've seen 'em somewhere, maybe up at Plaino. I know I've seen that skinny one with the scar."

"Wouldn't be surprised if you have," Slade replied. "Let's see what they've got on them. Might tie up with something. A couple of you jiggers scout around through the brush and see if any horses were left behind. They might tie up with somebody."

The pockets turned out a miscellany of objects including knives, keys, various knick-knacks and considerable money, none of which Slade deemed of significance. The pockets themselves interested him, however.

"What do you make of this dust caked in the lining seams?" he asked Mason.

The big puncher dug out some and rubbed it between his thumb and forefinger. "Alkali dust or something mighty like it," was his decision.

"And where do you find alkali dust around here?" Slade asked.

"Only on that danged desert down to the southwest," said Mason. "Ride out there an hour and you're powdered with it, and it seeps into everything. But these hellions must have prowled around there considerable to get a collection like this in their pockets."

Slade nodded. He held a similar opinion.

"What will we do with the carcasses?" asked Mason.

"We'll pack them in the chuckwagon and take to Lucas and turn them over to the sheriff," Slade decided. "I believe we're still in Yoakum County or close enough to it to pretend we are. Anyhow I figure they should be put on exhibition in Lucas. If you boys figure you saw them somewhere, it's pretty sure somebody in Lucas will recognize them."

"Makes sense," Mason agreed. "Here come the conductor and the rear brakeman—I see their lanterns. I told the boys to stay back there till I showed up."

The conductor and the head brakeman were in a state of great excitement but otherwise all right.

"I sent Hardesty back to flag anything that might come along, although I don't think anything will for a couple of hours," said the conductor. He gestured to his companion. "This work-dodger should have been riding on top of the cars, according to regulations, instead of being holed up in the caboose, but maybe it's lucky he wasn't."

"I've a notion you're right," Slade agreed. "He'd have been a tempting target up there. Can you fellows take the train in?"

"Sure," the conductor replied. "The fireman can handle the throttle and Ted here can shovel coal."

"Okay," Slade said. "We'll help the engineer down from the cab and you can stop the caboose here long enough to pick him up and give him a chance to lie down. He isn't hurt much but a forty-five slug packs a devil of a wallop and he's pretty well shook up. Get him to a doctor as soon as you pull in."

The fireman filled his tank with water and the train pulled out, pausing long enough to place the injured engineer in the caboose and then roaring eastward.

"And now we'll pick up our souvenirs and head for camp," Slade said. "Reckon we can pack 'em behind the saddles for that distance. Pity you jiggers couldn't find their horses. Guess they either followed the others when they lit out or got scared and hightailed off somewhere. Doesn't matter. Let's go. We can all do with a few hours of sleep and get an early start back to the spread."

With extra horses from the remuda hitched to the chuck wagon, the trip back to the Flying W was made easily the following day, the grim cavalcade arriving at the ranchhouse before dark. There the bodies were given a once-over and several of the hands expressed the opinion that they had seen one or more of them at Plaino or someplace.

"I was sure you'd get the herd through all right but I never expected anything as good as this," old Tom declared exultantly. "A little more of it and we're liable to have peace hereabouts. You're sure thinning them out. You ought to be sheriff of the county. You've done more to clean up things in a couple of weeks than that terrapin-brain who's supposed to be sheriff has done since he took office."

"He'll get a chance to see what he can do tomorrow," Slade predicted. "We'll pack the bodies to town in the morning, and

I want you and Dobie and Mason and two or three of the boys to go along. It's about time folks in this section were getting together and understanding one another better."

"Reckon that sort of makes sense," Wardell conceded. "Sure we'll go along."

CHAPTER SIXTEEN

THERE WAS PLENTY OF EXCITEMENT in Lucas when the Flying W chuck wagon arrived the following morning with its grisly load. The bodies were laid out in the sheriff's office for inspection. Sheriff Sloan examined them and there was a strained expression on his face when he raised his eyes to Slade.

"Recognize them?" the Ranger asked.

"Yes, I do," Sloan replied slowly. "Slade, every one of these men worked for Bob Biggers of the Double B."

Slade nodded and didn't appear particularly surprised.

"And that means, I suppose, that Biggers is the outlaw Ellis Dawson," the sheri continued.

"Possibly," Slade replied without enthusiasm.

The sheriff's face turned grim. "Then I'm riding out to the Double B right now to drop a loop on him and the rest of his hellions," he declared. "Will you come along?"

"Oh, sure, we'll all come along," Slade answered noncommittally.

Sheriff Sloan shot him an exasperated glance. "Haven't you got nerve in your body?" he demanded. "You sure don't seem a bit excited about it."

"I'm not," Slade said, "because I'm willing to bet a hatful of pesos that when we get to the Double B we won't find anybody."

"You mean he'll have pulled out?" exclaimed Sloan.

"Rather logical to assume so, don't you think?" Slade countered. "He'd hardly stick around knowing that the men downed in the course of the raid on the stock train would be brought here and looked over. But we'll ride out there and see what we can learn."

They learned very little. When they arrived at the Double B ranchhouse they found it deserted and plenty of signs of a hurried departure on the part of the occupants. The sheriff swore lurid oaths, ably abetted by Wardell and the Flying W hands. Slade ordered the cowboys to ride around the range a bit. They were back within an hour with a gloomy report.

"Don't believe there's fifty head of stock left on the spread," said Curly Mason. "They sure took the cows with them."

"Which was to be expected," Slade told him.

"But where the devil did they take them?" the baffled sheriff wanted to know.

"And I ain't got the answer," Sloan growled. "Oh, dang it, let's get back to town. Anyhow, we've got rid of the pest, which is something. Guess that washes up Ellis Dawson in this section."

Walt Slade didn't think so but refrained from arguing the point.

Dusk was falling when the disgruntled sheriff and his posse got back to Lucas. After stabling their horses they repaired to the First Chance for something to eat. The news of the recent happenings had spread like wildfire and was evidently the chief topic of conversation in the saloon. Big Val Russell, the Circle K owner, spotted them when they entered and came lumbering over to congratulate Slade.

"Bob Biggers!" he said, shaking his head sadly. "Always seemed to be a pretty good sort. Just goes to show you never can tell."

Tom Wardell and his men were introduced. Russell shook hands all around. Other prominent cattlemen joined the group and Wardell was soon discussing range matters with him in a friendly fashion. Slade also noted with satisfaction that the Flying W hands were mingling with punchers from the outfits to the east and south.

"Anyhow, it looks like we won't have a range war," he remarked to Sheriff Sloan who was brooding over his drink.

"Which is something," agreed Sloan. "Let's get a bite to eat."

They found a vacant table and sat down, giving their order to a waiter. The sheriff was silent for some minutes, then he suddenly burst out, "Slade, I've got a notion you don't believe Biggers is Ellis Dawson."

El Hacon smiled. "Well, to tell the truth I don't think he is," he admitted.

"Which means that Dawson is somebody else!" snorted the sheriff.

"A fairly obvious conclusion," Slade agreed with another smile.

"Oh, you know what I mean," growled Sloan. "I mean Dawson is somebody else hanging around this section. Is that what you believe?"

"Yes," Slade replied simply.

"Then where does Biggers come in?" asked the bewildered sheriff.

"Biggers was working with him, that's all," Slade said. Biggers had to cut and run for it, but Dawson is still around, all right. And don't be too sure you're finished with him. In my opinion you're not. Biggers was merely in the nature of a hired hand carrying out orders, with Dawson doing the thinking. He's a shrewd article and absolutely snake-blooded. If he concludes Biggers is all of a sudden a liability, you won't have to worry about Biggers any more. Dawson will see that he's taken care of. However, I don't believe Dawson will figure that way, not just yet at any rate. Having successfully gotten in the clear, Biggers is still useful to him and he's a bit short of hands right now."

"But if Biggers isn't Dawson, who the devil is?" worried the sheriff.

"Still an unanswered question," Slade returned.

"Do you think he's liable to bust loose someplace else soon?"

"I'm inclined to believe so," Slade conceded. "The question is, where? I've a notion he'll lay off cattle for a while. Having recently lost nine of his men I doubt if he has enough left to handle a big widelooping chore. Not that he'll have any trouble getting more in a hurry. An outlaw of his standing can always round up new recruits when he needs them. But I think you can rely on him pulling something before long, if he isn't stopped."

"Now I am worried," lamented Sloan. "There's an election coming up next month and if Dawson is still sashaying around then there'll be a new face in the sheriff's office sure as blazes. I only hope," he added with a boyish grin, "that you don't take a notion to run against me. You'd win hands down."

"You can rest easy on that score," Slade laughed.

Wardell and Dobie came over to the table and the discussion ended.

It was late when they got back to the Flying W ranch-house but old Tom seemed to be in a mood for conversation.

"Russell and a couple more of those fellers are riding up tomorrow to have a look at what John got from crossing Anguses and Herefords with longhorns and then cross-breeding again," he observed suddenly. "They seemed sort of interested. Funny, ain't it, this time last month I reckon the only way they'd have rode up was packing saddle guns."

"Notions can change mighty fast," Slade commented.

"Yes, when somebody takes a hand in the changing," Wardell replied dryly.

He paused, looking contemplative. "Slade," he resumed, "the first day you showed up here I had a little talk with old Manuel, the cook. He seemed to know considerable about you."

"That so?" Slade nodded, with a smile.

"Uh-huh, that's so," said old Tom. "He had quite a few things to say, all of 'em good, but one in particular sort of stuck in my mind. I couldn't get it out and as the days jogged along I kept thinking of it more and more till I pretty well decided that Manuel sure had the right notion."

"Yes?" Slade prompted.

"He said," old Tom pronounced slowly, "that you go about doing good."

Slade's expression was abruptly very serious and there was no laughter in his steady eyes.

"I only hope he's right," he said.

"I've a plumb solid notion that he is," Wardell declared emphatically. "Since you showed up here things have changed one devil of a lot, and I'm sure for certain they're going to keep on changing for the better. Son, how in blazes do you do it?"

"Mr. Wardell," Slade replied, "I've learned by experience that most of the trouble in the world is caused by wrong conceptions about our fellowmen. Once those misapprehensions are cleared up we usually find that on the average they are much like ourselves and with more good than bad in their make-up. There are exceptions, of course, but I believe that generally speaking the rule holds good. Here in this section, due to a misunderstanding, there has been the makings of bad trouble. Now that understanding has taken over it's highly unlikely that there'll be any trouble. I don't think you have a desire any longer to throw lead at Val Russell, and his associates for instance, any more than they hold any grudge against you. I can't see any reason why the present condition shouldn't continue, can you?"

"I sure can't," admitted Wardell, "and I feel one sight better about it. Holding grudges is bad for the digestion."

"Both physical and spiritual," Slade smiled.

Old Tom regarded him gravely for a moment. "You're a funny feller, son," he said at length. "I'm old enough to be your dad, almost your granddad, but sometimes you make me feel like a little boy."

Slade laughed outright. "I've often wondered if years really have much to do with age," he returned lightly.

"I don't know about that," admitted Wardell, "but I do know that they make the bones ache if you stay up too late. I'm going to bed."

Slade spent the following day attending to various range chores. He returned to the ranchhouse in the late afternoon for something to eat and a little rest, but shortly after dusk found him in the saddle again, riding east by slightly north, toward where Carter Renshaw's gaily painted ranchhouse sat near the north-south trail.

Slade was convinced that Renshaw and not Bob Biggers was the outlaw Ellis Dawson, but he was forced to admit that his belief was based on very flimsy evidence, the phony quarrel between Renshaw and Biggers in the First Chance and the sign-board at the edge of the desert painted the same colors as those with which Renshaw had seen fit to decorate his ranchhouse. Not much to go on, but Slade was following a hunch.

His chief worry was that Renshaw had pulled out with Biggers. If he had, the hunt must go on. There was little likelihood that he would remain anywhere in the vicinity if he had decided to cut and run, and Texas was a dang big state. He would bob up somewhere, of course, but would be able to raise plenty of trouble before Slade managed to get a line on him again.

But if Renshaw hadn't pulled out, Slade felt pretty sure that Biggers would not be far off, either. He would have holed up somewhere waiting for orders from the boss.

Slade based his hopes chiefly on the premise that Renshaw would have no reason to believe he was suspect, especially with attention centered on Biggers. Well, he'd try and find out. Settling himself in the saddle he rode steadily at a good pace until he knew the ranchhouse could be no great distance off, then slowed Shadow to a little better than a walk. There was no moon but the night was clear, the sky brilliant with stars. By their wan glow objects were visible for a considerable distance.

It was the gray ribbon of the trail, shimmering faintly in the starlight which warned Slade that he was approaching the ranchhouse. A few minutes later he saw its shadowy bulk. He uttered an exclamation of satisfaction. A light glowed behind a window.

But the paramount question still remained, was Renshaw there? Slade felt he had to make sure. But how? He earnestly desired to get a look into that lighted room, but getting it was considerable of a problem. Between where he sat his horse and the ranchhouse was a wide stretch of open prairie. Even in the dim starlight anybody riding across it would be clearly visible from the ranchhouse were someone keeping watch. And a man in such a position as Slade believed Renshaw to be might very well be much on his guard. He glanced around in search of a solution to the problem.

A couple of hundred yards to the south was a scattering of trees. It was black dark under their spreading branches. He turned Shadow's head and rode until he reached the shelter of the grove. There he dismounted, removed the bit so the horse could graze and dropped the split reins to the ground, a warning to Shadow not to move about too much. Confident that the black wouldn't stray, he walked to the edge of the trees and gazed toward the ranchhouse. He could plainly see the golden rectangle of the window. The glow blurred from time to time as if somebody inside the house had walked between it and the light.

The needle grass that carpeted the prairie was tall, the amber heads reaching nearly to Slade's waist. He decided that by assuming a crouch he would be almost invisible in the dim light. With a final glance around he headed for the ranchhouse. His progress slow and painful. Soon his back ached and his legs were cramped from the awkward position, but he grimly persisted until he was within a few yards of the trail. There he stretched out on the ground for a few minutes to ease his strained muscles and considered the situation.

It was not very satisfactory. He would have to cross the trail and then there remained some thirty or forty yards of open space. If anybody was keeping watch in or outside the ranchhouse, doubtless his first intimation of the fact would be the crack of a gun he wouldn't hear, lead travelling a bit faster than sound. For long minutes he crouched in the grass, studying the prospect from every angle. Nothing moved outside the building, so far as he could see, nor inside it either, for that matter. Only the steady glow of the lighted window persisted. It seemed to beckon him to come forward and learn what it would reveal, and at the same time to warn him that what he contemplated was a risky business. He could see now that the window was located near one corner of the house, around which he could not see.

Finally the dubious invitation of the glowing square grew too strong. He straightened into his crouch and slid across the gray expanse of the trail as quickly as he could. He breathed a little easier when he reached the grass-grown ranchhouse yard. It was a bit darker here and if he hadn't been spotted crossing the trail he felt he quite likely wouldn't be in the deeper gloom. Anyhow he was in for it; no sense in holding back further. With quick, light steps he stole forward till he was crouched beneath the window. Listening intently, he could hear a rumble of voices but could not make out what was said. Slowly, cautiously, careful not to make the slightest sound, he straightened until he could peer over the window sill.

For a moment his eyes were dazzled by the light, then they focused on the occupants of the room, three men seated at a table. He instantly recognized all three. Two lanky individuals had been members of the group of five who had accompanied Carter Renshaw the night he had the staged run-in with Bob Biggers. The third member of the trio was Renshaw himself.

Renshaw was talking earnestly to his companions, gesturing with his hands, his dark eyes glowing. He looked to be in a bad temper about something. His companions wore a sullen expression and Slade surmised that Renshaw was telling them off for some reason or other. But he could not catch what was said through the closed window. Well anyhow he had learned what he had come to learn, that Renshaw hadn't pulled out with Biggers, so he had better get in the clear while he had the chance. He took a step back, straightened up and turned, just as a man loomed around the corner of the house. He caught the gleam of upraised steel and dived forward frantically as the knife swept down.

It was the vicious force of the blow that saved him. The knife point ripped through the muscle over his shoulder blade, but the man's wrist came down on the top of his shoulder with such numbing violence that his hand flew open and the knife fell to the ground. For an instant he staggered off balance. Before he could recover Slade's corded left arm was about his throat, his right hand gripped over his mouth and chin.

In grim silence save for the hissing of their breath they struggled. The fellow tore at Slade's wrist with both hands but couldn't break his hold. He brought his knee up hard, but Slade blocked the foul blow with his own thigh. His voice gutteralled in his throat but couldn't get past the hand clamped over his mouth. Slade knew that one yell from him and the men in the room would be out with guns blazing. Something had to be done in a hurry. He put forth every atom of his strength in a wrenching sideways twist, his arm levered against the other's throat, his right hand jerking his chin around and up.

There was a soft crackling sound, as of a wet stick snapping. The man's boot heels beat a queer, muffled tattoo on the turf, his body jerked spasmodically and then went limp, as Slade eased off a little on his chin, his head lolled sideways in a hideous fashion. Slade's breath caught in his throat. With that sudden terrific wrench he had broken the fellow's neck.

For a moment Slade stood rigid, breathing in short gasps and holding the flaccid body erect. The rumble of talk, still muffled inside the building. Evidently the small sounds of the struggle under the window had not been heard by the occupants of the room. He eased the body to the ground and glided away from the ranchhouse, increasing his speed as soon as he had crossed the trail. A few minutes more and he was in the saddle and riding west. He couldn't get away from that devilish build-ing fast enough. His gashed shoulder ached and burned and the inside of his shirt was a disagreeable warm stickiness, but he gave small thought to mere physical discomforts at the moment. The savage death grapple and its dreadful finish had shaken him no little. The aftermath was nauseating. To make matters worse, a sudden disquieting uneasiness had gripped him. Suppose he was wrong about Renshaw. Then the man he killed with his hands could well have been but an honest cowboy who saw him crouched beneath the window and believed he had murderous designs on the occupants of the room. The thought was not pleasant.

His mind was eased a bit, however, as he recalled the vicious stealthiness of the attack. The fellow had been out to kill and without warning, whereas the instinctive reaction of an honest man would have been to jam a gun in his back and ask what the devil he was doing there.

Well, the matter would have to be brought to a head and without delay. Slade had a theory and resolved to test it out at the first opportunity. He hoped his injury would not hold him back.

After what seemed an eternity of painful riding he reached the Flying W. He got the rig off Shadow and rubbed him down as best he could. Then he headed for the ranchhouse where a low light burned in the living room. Abruptly he was not feeling at all good. He entered and sank wearily in a chair dropping his head in his hands.

There was a light patter of small bare feet on the stairs and Dolores was beside him.

"Heavens above! Now what?" she asked.

Slade raised his head and grinned at her, a bit wanly. "I won't argue about you taking a look at this one," he said. "I don't think it amounts to much but it's where I can't see it."

She helped him to remove his blood soaked shirt and examined the wound.

"An ugly cut but fortunately it's not very deep," she decided. "I'll cleanse it and draw the edges together with plaster and it should be all right. Lucky I've had so much experience from patching up Dad and Tom and the boys. You'd keep a doctor busy full time."

She went to work on the wound with her deft and soothing fingers. A little later she draped his shirt around his shoulders and stepped back.

"That should do it," she said. "Now tell me what happened."

Slade decided it was best to tell her everything and proceeded to do so.

"Carter Renshaw," she said thoughtfully when he had finished. "He visited here a few times. He's pleasant, courteous, well spoken and appears to have better than average educacation, but just the same, I never liked him. Call it woman's intuition again, if you will, but somehow he always repelled me. Perhaps it's his dead looking eyes. They give me the creeps."

"I think I understand," Slade said soberly. "Say! you've got that shoulder feeling a devil of a lot better. Now I'm ready for anything."

CHAPTER SEVENTEEN

SLADE AWOKE LATE THE NEXT MORNING with a sore shoulder and a stiff arm, but otherwise feeling okay. He spent the rest of the day loafing around the ranchhouse and its environs and talking with Dolores. Old Tom and his son had ridden off somewhere and didn't return till late.

By evening Slade decided he was in condition for a little riding himself. He saddled up and rode south through Skull Canyon.

The sinister gorge was a disquieting place at night, with shadows curdling in its depths and the rimrock glowing with star shine. The wind whispered mournfully through the leaves and night birds added their eerie cries to intensify the air of bleak desolation that hung over the canyon like a poisonous miasma over a deathly swamp. Now and then Slade caught sight of a wan glow in some thicket or clump of grass, the phosphorescent gleam of decaying bones. Once a panther screamed somewhere in the black depths, like the despairing wail of a spirit damned to wander timelessly through the shadows, seeking frantically for companionship and finding none. Slade could understand how the weird legends dealing with the ominous ravine had birthed and grown throughout the years. He was not much bothered with nerves but just the same he experienced a sense of relief when he left the south mouth and rode at a faster pace south by west across the prairie. He reached the great buffalo track and turned into it. He would have liked to examine the mysterious signboard again but it was too dark to locate it, so he continued until he drew rein at the edge of the desert.

Before him stretched the arid wastelands, gleaming faintly in the silvery sheen and looking as solemn and quiet and alien to man as the star-studded firmament above.

On the prairie the night had been cool, but here a hot breath fanned Slade's cheek, the dreaded furnace wind that often roared across the desert during the dark hours to raise the powdered sand and the alkali dust in blinding clouds.

"Suppose we see what it's like out there?" he suggested to Shadow. The black horse snorted dubiously but obediently moved forward.

Before he had covered a mile Slade realized that the dangers of the wasteland had not been exaggerated. Even at night the heat was oppressive and the dust made him cough. Shadow's hoofs slogged laboriously through the powdery stuff that formed the desert's floor and his progress was slow.

"It's bad, feller, but you ain't seen nothin' yet," Slade told him as he turned back to the prairie. "Next trip we'll be ready to make a real try at it. I'm pretty sure it can be done, but we'll have to start not so long before dawn. No sense in groping around out here in the dark. What we're looking for, if it really does exist, will take daylight to find."

He returned to the ranchhouse, arriving there a couple of hours before daylight, and immediately went to bed.

Slade had been somewhat comforted by Dolores' appraisal of Carter Renshaw, for he had great faith in the natural instincts of women and horses, especially where men were concerned, but he knew the crawling uneasiness that had afflicted him since the fight under the window would not be wholly allayed until he had definitely proven that Carter was Ellis Dawson.

That afternoon Slade made careful preparations for his trip across the dread Tucumcari Desert. He procured two canteens, filled them with water and stored them in his saddle pouches, along with some staple provisions for he did not know how long he might have to wander the wasteland. He made sure that Shadow's hoofs and legs were in perfect condition, the irons tightly affixed, with no loose nails. His life could easily depend on the strength and sagacity of his horse.

Old Tom was highly dubious about the adventure when Slade confided in him what he had in mind.

"You'll be taking a devil of a chance, son," he protested. "I don't see why you have to risk it."

"It's my job," Slade replied simply. He slipped something from a cunningly concealed secret pocket in his broad leather belt and laid it on the table between them. It was the famous silver star set on a silver circle, the feared and honored badge of the Texas Rangers.

Wardell stared at the symbol of law and order hated by the outlaw fraternity and admired and respected by honest men.

"Might have known it," he said. "In fact, I've kinda suspected something of this sort for quite a while, and I'm pretty sure Sime Dobie has known it all along. Yes, I guess it's your job, all right. Well, I've a notion you'll come out on top. The Rangers usually do."

"Usually, but not always," Slade qualified, "but Ellis Dawson is a bit of unfinished business and having taken cards in the game, I'll have to play out the hand."

"Here's hoping you corner the jackpot," said Wardell, "but I still think you oughta take somebody with you, me or Curly Mason, for instance. If it comes to a showdown you could stand a little backing."

"Thanks, sir," Slade replied, "but I've a notion one man by himself will have a better chance of getting through than several."

As he spoke he pinned the silver star on his shirt front. "Guess there's no sense in keeping under cover any longer," he observed. "And this thing does pack considerable weight. Unless a fellow is in mighty deep he's not likely to pull on it."

In the dark hour of midnight Slade again took the eerie ride through Skull Canyon. There would be a late moon but as yet the gloom was deep.

"Horse, we're gambling," he told Shadow. "Gambling on the guess that out there near the middle of the desert is water and a place where cows can be held during the hot hours. If I'm right we may get a chance to clean up this mess. If I'm wrong, this time tomorrow night you and I will very likely know a lot of things we don't know now, including what is the meaning of this show called life and where it leads to."

As he rode, Slade wondered what Carter Renshaw had thought when he discovered the dead man with a broken neck under his ranchhouse window. If Renshaw really was Dawson it must have thrown a devil of a scare into him, and might well expedite his flight from the section, in which event, there was no time to waste. Slade instinctively quickened Shadow's pace.

Slade knew very well that in venturing onto the desert as he intended he was risking his life. That it could be crossed by a mounted man had been proven, but that meant riding mostly during the somewhat cooler night hours and not fooling on the way. To pause to prowl around in the middle of it under the blazing sun was altogether different matter. It would have been more discreet to wait for a day of rain or clouds, but that would have minimized his chances of finding what he sought. Besides, the uneasy feeling that time was running short persisted. So he resolved to take the desperate chance and hope for the best.

The moon was peeping over the edge of the world when he reached the old bison trail. After considerable searching he found the strange signboard and studied it by the strengthening moonlight and a match or two. The message it intended to convey was, Slade thought, fairly obvious: the kettle over the fire said that water was to be had nearby; the two men squatting beside it told that there was a favorable spot for a camp; the man riding out of the east indicated that the spot could be readily reached by a horseman, even in the daytime, for the sun was shown over-head. The arrow pointing toward what was undoubtedly a rock formation—the desert was dotted with such—signified that the formation was important, presumably the source of the water. All to a certain extent guesswork, he had to admit, but he felt that he had read the thing right.

Squatting behind the bone, he sighted across the broad, sharp-edged blade. The line of his vision rested on a high flat-topped mountain that he knew must be well beyond the New Mexico state line. The peak was prominent, taller than those on either side, and would provide a landmark for anybody desir-ing to cross the desert in line with the direction indicated by the blade, but a very little deviation to either side would bring one far of the mark. He studied the distant peak that glowed coldly in the moonlight. The bone pointed to the exact middle of the flat top. Shouldn't be too hard to ride a straight course with that kept in mind. That is if one of the infernal dust storms didn't come up all of a sudden and blot out the mountain and everything else. That chance he had to take, along with quite a few others equally as hazardous or more so. Mounting Shadow he rode west along the broad track.

At the edge of the desert he hesitated a little, as one is apt to do before taking an irrevocable step. Then with a shrug of his broad shoulders he sent Shadow out onto the deathly desolation.

Even in the comparative cool of the night the heat was oppressive, the dust choking and terrible. The furnace wind blew out from the west and stirred the powdery surface in strangling clouds that caused both horse and man to cough and sneeze con-tinually. Often the distant peak that was their guide was com-pletely obscured, but when the wind lulled a bit the dust sank and its mighty bulk became visible. And Slade knew that the night wind caused by the heat rising from the desert floor and the cool air rushing down from the mountains invariably sank with the dawn. What he had to fear after the coming of daylight was a sudden storm sweeping up from the south.

The eastern sky was flushing rose and gold and the wind was dying when Slade pulled Shadow to a halt on the lip of a vast depression in the desert floor, eyeing it dubiously. He didn't like the looks of it one bit, but dared not risk a detour, not knowing how great might be its extent. He sent the black horse down the gently sloping side.

The great hollow was indeed a terrible place. The silence could almost be heard, and its wide floor had the appearance of being sifted with the dust of dessicated bones. It was a fitting place for Death to have his ghastly throne of bleached skulls. The moonlight and the strengthening bloom in the east glowed about its rim but the shadow seemed loath to depart from its depths. And when at last light flowed in a flood over the eastern edge the whole great surface of the amphitheatre gleamed and sparkled like a vast robe sewn with pearls.

"I'd say down here is quite likely a massive sedimentary bed of gypsum," he told Shadow. "I wouldn't be surprised if some day folks are liable to wake up to the fact that this section of what appears to be worthless wasteland is quite valuable. Well, any jigger who sets out to work it will sure earn what he gets.

"And I wouldn't be surprised," he added, "if it was somewhere around here that Val Russell's range boss was killed. This hole is a perfect set-up for a mirage. The air down here is heated tremendously and becomes much more rarefied than the air even a few feet above the lip of the basin. The rays arriving from a distant object in a nearly horizontal but slightly downward direction can't penetrate into the lighter air but are reflected upward by the boundary and to anyone standing over the edge of the desert, the images would seem to be suspended in midair, as I saw them. Funny how things work out. I reckon there is always an 'eye' on what we do that we shouldn't."

Shadow nodded his head gravely as if understanding perfectly this scientific and mystical analysis of the phenomenon.
Slade chuckled and rode on through the growing heat. Finally
they worked their way out of the ghastly hole and continued west.

But now the sun was well above the horizon and the heat
growing more terrible by the minute. Slade began doling out
his precious water to his horse and to himself. If they had followed their desires, they would have emptied both canteens in
the first hour. It was not only the blistering heat that dried their
throats. The alkali dust was frightfully irritating to the mucous
membranes. Soon Slade's lips were cracked and bleeding and his
nostrils itched and burned. Altogether he was experiencing the
exact sensations one would attribute to a beefsteak or a gridiron.
He was literally being baked through and through and the burning sun seemed to be sucking his very blood out of him. Nowhere
in sight was a rock or a tree, nothing but an unending glare, ren-
dered dazzling by the hot air which danced over the surface of
the desert as it does over a red-hot stove.

"We can't stand much more of this," he muttered to Shadow
who plodded wearily on, his head drooping, his tongue hanging
out between his blackened lips.

Slade stared with bloodshot eyes at the distant mountain that
was his only guide across this inferno of heat and dust. Although
he had been riding for hours it seemed no nearer than when he
started. Rocks were beginning to appear, now, buttes and spires
and fantastically carved columns, but none of them resembling
the fortress-like bulk depicted on the signboard. He wondered
dully if the dang thing had really followed the Indian tradition
and pointed the correct direction with the blade of the bone. He
had surmised that it did if he was wrong he might be miles off
the true course.

A little later he halted Shadow and dismounted stiffly. He
poured the last of the water from his first canteen and half the
contents of the second into his hat and let the patient animal have

a good drink. Then he moistened his own cracked lips and swallowed a few drops. He mounted again and Shadow, somewhat revived, shambled on a little faster.

It was well past mid-morning and Slade was growing distinctly uneasy when he came to the lip of another of the deathly depressions, wider and deeper than the previous one. He pulled Shadow to a halt, hesitating to risk entering this super-inferno that lay before him. But the great sink extended north and south as far as the eye could reach, effectually barring his path toward the distant peak that was his guide. He decided it was better to trust himself to its ghastly depths than to attempt to detour it. By doing so he would very likely lose sight of the landmark upon which he depended. He sent Shadow down the crumbly slope. Finally he reached the terrible bottom of the bowl which appeared to be miles in extent. His uneasiness grew to near panic as he used up the last of the water now heated to about the same temperature as a man's blood.

And then, when he was about ready to give in to despair, he saw, still far ahead and a little to the north what looked to be a huge fortress rising mountain-like from the floor of the bowl. Staring at it, he experienced a surge of relief. The massive rock formation certainly bore a marked resemblance to the painting. He doubted if there could be two such outcroppings in the desert.

But the terrific heat was still increasing, the mass of rock grew misty and distorted to Slade's gaze. His eyes burned, the blood hammered at his temples and a great bell seemed to be tolling in his head. Shadow's sides were heaving, spasmodic shiverings rippled his dust powdered hide. Slade knew that both he and the horse were very close to the limit of their endurance. Maybe they had enough left to make it, but he wasn't sure.

CHAPTER EIGHTEEN

NEARER AND NEARER LOOMED THE ROCK, its dark sides reflecting the rays of the sun, its towering pinnacles reaching toward the brassy sky. Now it hung directly over him, the heat beating back from it in scorching waves. Shadow struggled along its curving base until the trend of its rugged side turned from north to west. Slade straightened in his saddle, then with bewildering speed he hurled himself sideways from the hull, sliding his Winchester from the boot as he fell. Apparently from the blank wall of rock a man had appeared, a gun in his hand. Even as Slade's body hit the sands a bullet yelled through the space it had occupied the instant before.

Flinging the rifle to his shoulder, Slade fired two quick shots under Shadow's belly. The gunman reeled, threw up his hands and pitched headlong onto the sands to lie writhing and moaning.

Slade leaped to his feet, rifle ready for instant action. The man's gun lay where it had fallen and its owner was evidently hard hit. Slade decided there was nothing more to fear from him. He advanced warily, the cocked Winchester at the ready. The fellow might have companions.

Apparently he didn't. Nobody else materialized like a ghost from the nothingness. But as Slade drew near he saw what he had previously missed. There was an opening in the cliff face, though one invisible from a few paces away since one outer edge projected slantingly over the inner wall of rock. The opening was some twenty feet wide by perhaps ten in height.

The man on the ground was still writhing and moaning, his face twisted and distorted by sharp agony. Slade set his rifle aside and knelt beside him.

"I'm dying!" the man gasped. "Help me! For God's sake do something for me!"

Slade examined the wound. He had gotten him through the chest but high up and well to one side. He decided it was not as bad as it appeared to be.

"Maybe I can do something for you—maybe stop you from bleeding to death," he told the fellow. "That is, if you'll answer a few questions."

"I'll answer," the other gasped, "just help me. I ain't ready to die!"

Slade went to work on him, padding and bandaging the wound to stop the flow of blood. From various indications he decided there was little if any internal bleeding. The fellow, he wasn't very old and didn't look too vicious, panted answers to the questions Slade put to him as he worked.

"Sure Renshaw is Ellis Dawson. Yes, that painted bone is to show us fellers who come up from the south for the cattle how to get here. We run 'em on across the infernal desert to Mexico to a buyer and then head 'em south and re-sell 'em to another buyer down there."

Slade nodded. He understood the set-up. Cattle stealing was big business that employed a highly efficient and carefully worked out organization. Dawson could sell all he rustled for ten dollars or better a head. The crooked dealer who bought from him would re-sell for fifteen and still leave a nice profit for the final purchaser. The system had the added advantage of keeping the stolen cows moving swiftly from hand to hand, the result, much more difficult to trace. Doubtless Dawson was able to really set up in business in this section from the proceeds of the three-thousand head shipping herd he widelooped from Tom Wardell in the course of the Nueces rancher's initial drive through the section. It would have enabled him to buy the small ranch that was an excellent cover-up for his activities.

"Dawson?" the wounded outlaw replied to another question. "He's supposed to show up here this evening with Bob Biggers. They aim to hole up here for a few days and then slip across into New Mexico and head south. No, I don't think there'll be anybody else with them. They ain't got but three or four fellers of their bunch left and they've already headed south and aim to scatter. They know you're on their trail and don't want no more of you. Water? Plenty of it back in the dang cave. Do you think you can drag me in out of the sun?"

"Reckon so," Slade replied. He picked up the man's bulky body, apparently without effort and, cradling him in his arms, entered the dark opening, Shadow clicking along behind him. Slade found himself in a corridor running through the rock.

"Straight ahead," mumbled the wounded outlaw. "Ain't nothing to fall over. You'll see light in a minute."

Slade did see light and a moment later entered a great cavern hollowed out, evidently by natural forces, in the heart of the rock. It was lighted by a blaze kindled in a rude stone fireplace and by several torches stuck in crevices in the wall. One whole side of the wide enclosure was fenced in by strands of barbed wire, forming an excellent corral. The cave was rank with the smell of cattle.

Several bunks were built along the near wall of the cave. On one of these Slade deposited his burden. Nearby a tethered horse contentedly munched oats.

"Right through that hole in the wall across there and you'll come to the water," mumbled the wounded man. "Bucket by the fire. I wish you'd bring me a little, too. I feel awful hot inside."

Slade nodded and procured the bucket, plucking one of the torches from the wall.

"Don't do any moving around," he warned the outlaw. "If you start that bleeding again you're a goner."

Confident that there was nothing to fear from the fellow, he entered the tunnel in the far wall, which had a sharp downward slope. He followed it for a hundred yards or so and heard the sound of running water. Another moment and he stood on the bank of a rushing stream of unknown width. The black water hissed smoothly at his feet, coming out of the darkness and vanishing into the darkness again, its surface gleaming in the torch light.

There was nothing particularly astonishing about it being here, Slade knew. There was a vast underground water system in this region and the tunnel merely tapped one of the web of streams that underlay the whole Staked Plains country including the desert. The Indians had known of it, of course, but had kept their secret. Dawson or somebody who relayed the information to him had discovered it, doubtless by chance.

Slade whistled Shadow who came pounding and snorting through the dark to plunge a grateful muzzle into the stream. Slade satisfied his own burning thirst then filled the bucket and returned to the main cave. He gave the wounded man a drink, rolled a cigarette and placed it between his lips. The man gave him a grateful look and puffed avidly. Abruptly he spoke.

"Just want to tell you something, feller," he said. "You may think I'm lying, but I ain't. I didn't see your star or I wouldn't have throwed down on you. I ain't much good, but I ain't shooting at no Rangers."

Slade believed him. "You say Dawson and Biggers are supposed to come here later in the day?" he asked.

"That's right," the other said. "They should make it in before dark. And listen, feller, you may not believe me, but I'm pulling for you to come out on top. That snake-eyed hellion wouldn't do anything for me. He'd just leave me here to die."

Slade felt he was very likely right.

"But look out for Dawson," the man warned. "He's plumb deadly with that sleeve gun he packs. I never saw a faster pull.

What you should do is hole up out there at the edge of the rock and mow 'em down with your long gun as soon as they show; that's what they'd do to you."

It was good advice, Slade had to admit, but the code of the Rangers wouldn't permit him to follow it. He was a peace officer and must conduct himself accordingly. Dawson and Biggers would be given a chance to surrender.

With plenty of time on his hands, Slade cooked a meal from the provisions with which the cave was stocked and made some broth for the wounded man. The fellow slept fitfully from time to time and toward evening was in less pain and appeared to have gained a little strength.

During the afternoon Slade made several trips to the outside, but each time nothing but the blazing, empty shimmer of the desert rewarded his gaze. It was close to sunset when he noted movement far out on the wasteland. It resolved to two horsemen riding steadily from the east. Slade took up his position just inside the fold of rock and waited. As the two riders drew near he recognized Bob Biggers and Carter Renshaw. He waited until they were within twenty paces and then stepped into view.

His voice rang out, "Elevate! In the name of the State of Texas! You are under arrest!"

The outlaws jerked their horses to a stop, staring at the tall form of El Halcon with the star of the Rangers gleaming on his broad breast. Under the threat of his gun muzzle they slowly raised their arms. Biggers' eyes goggled, his mouth hung open. Renshaw's handsome face was a mask of fury.

Slade's eyes never left Renshaw's right hand. He was ready when it darted forward like the head of a striking snake. His Colt wisped smoke the instant before the stubby derringer boomed.

Renshaw reeled sideways and fell, a blue hole between his glaring eyes. Biggers jerked his gun and got in one shot that fanned Slade's face before he died with the Ranger's two bullets laced through his heart.

Slade walked slowly forward and gazed down at the dead faces. Then he looped the horses' bridles over his arm and led them into the cave.

The wounded man had raised himself on his elbow. "Did you get 'em?" he asked eagerly.

"Yes," Slade replied and began taking the rigs off the horses. The outlaw sighed deeply and eased himself back on the bunk.

As soon as they were freed of their equipment, the horses, evidently familiar with their surroundings, trotted down the far passage to drink. Slade dished out oats for them from a sack and left them to their own devices, knowing that they would have no trouble making their way back to the grassland. He speculated the man on the bunk a moment.

"Feller," he said, "let's see if you can stand up and take a step or two. Take it slow and easy, now."

The other obeyed, easing himself to the floor. He wavered a little on his feet but took a couple of steps without difficulty.

"Okay," Slade said. "Sit down again and listen. I believe you can ride. You won't enjoy it particularly but I believe you can. I did the best I could for you but I'm not a doctor and I don't know what's going on inside of you. I think you should see a doctor as quickly as possible. I don't believe the ride will kill you, but if we stay here I can't answer for what might happen. What do you say, are you willing to take a chance?"

"I'll take it," the other replied.

"How does your side feel?" Slade asked.

"Not too bad," the man said. "Burns a bit but not as bad as it did. I believe you've got the right notion, feller. I'll make out."

"All right," Slade nodded. "I'll tie your legs to the stirrup straps against the chance of you tumbling out of the hull and you can sort of lean forward against the horse's neck. I'll lead him."

With Slade's help he managed to mount his horse. Slade lashed his legs loosely to the straps.

"That should hold you okay," he said. "How do you feel?"

"Not bad," the man replied. "Anyhow I'll be glad to get out of this dark hole. If I've got to cash in I'd rather do it under the sky."

Slade dragged the bodies of Renshaw and Biggers into the cave and left them there. It would be foolhardy to try to take them to town with him. He was liable to be in for enough trouble as it was.

In the deepening dusk they began the long ride. It was cooler at night although the furnace wind was already beginning to moan from the west and Slade felt they had a good chance to get across the desert before the sun rose, if the weather behaved itself.

The weather didn't and before they were twenty miles out on the wasteland Slade wished they had remained in the cave. With the furnace wind from the west steadily gaining strength, a second and much more violent wind roared up from the south, blistering hot, stirring the sands and raising the bitter alkali dust in clouds that at times completely obscured the stars. Slade hoped that his instinct for direction would hold them on the right course but there was always the terrible danger of becoming confused and riding aimlessly in a circle as many a lost traveller had done, to his death.

"But I think old Shadow will keep headed right," he told his companion.

Fiercer and fiercer grew the storm. The night was a gray inferno of heat and dust. The water they had brought with them was soon exhausted and men and beasts began to suffer frightfully from thirst. And still the weird vista unfolded before them. Strain their eyes as they would, they could catch no welcome glimpse of the grassland that they hoped lay somewhere ahead. Despite his confidence in Shadow's instinct for direction, Slade had to admit to himself that he was growing a bit panicky. He had faced death too many times to fear it particularly, but such a death of horror that threatened was enough to shake the strongest nerves. His mind was becoming foggy, there was a queer singing in his ears and a fluttering throb at his temples that hinted at erratic heart action. Once he felt himself slipping from the saddle and only saved himself by a frantic clutch at the horn. He knew that if he had fallen it was highly unlikely that he would have ever risen again.

Abruptly he was aware that the wounded man, slumped forward on his horse's neck, was gabbling something at him. He reined in and drew the lead horse abreast of Shadow. And the spark of good found in the most unexpected places flared up brightly.

"Listen, feller," the outlaw croaked, "with that good horse you can make it alone. If you stick with me we'll both take the big jump. Go on and leave me. No sense in both of us cashing in."

Slade's cracked lips widened in a smile. "We'll make it together or not at all," he said, and sent Shadow forward again.

The incident had a decidedly uplifting effect on the Ranger. All of a sudden he was imbued by an intense desire to get his wounded companion through safely. As a result he shook off the deadly lethargy that had been shrouding him. He straightened in the saddle, set his jaw grimly and doggedly fought the storm.

Somehow the dreadful night drew to a close. The wind let down a little as the stars began to pale. Abruptly the air cleared like magic and before them lay the emerald billows of the rangeland gleaming in the strengthening light of dawn.

"We made it!" Slade told his companion, who raised his haggard face from the horse's mane and grinned wanly.

Slade headed for a water hole that he knew was located a few miles to the northeast. Upon reaching it he got his companion from the saddle and stretched him out on the grass and gave him a good drink. After allowing the horses as much water as he thought good for them he removed the bits and turned them loose to graze.

"We'll rest here till the sun's well up and give the critters a chance to catch their wind," he said. "Then we should be able to make it to town okay."

Lucas seethed with excitement when Slade rode in with his prisoner. Sheriff Sloan shook his head as he stared at the Ranger star on Slade's breast.

"Reckon I should have guessed it, but I didn't," he said.

"Help me get this gent in where he can lie down," Slade directed. "A bunk in one of the cells back of your office will do for the time being, then send for a doctor to look him over."

"What charge are you putting against him?" asked the sheriff.

"None, I guess," Slade replied. "He isn't so bad and he didn't really belong to Dawson's bunch. I think he'll ride a straight trail from now on."

"You're darn right," the prisoner gulped gratefully. "I've sure learned my lesson and I'll never mix up with anything off-color again as long as I live."

"Don't," Slade advised. "That kind of a trail leads to only one end, and it isn't a nice one." He sat down wearily and rolled a cigarette.

"Yes, Renshaw and Biggers had a nice system worked out," he told Sloan. "Biggers handled the widelooping down here and Renshaw worked on the Nueces folks up to the north, meanwhile striving very subtly to keep the Nueces people and the folks down here on the prod against one another."

"Funny though, wasn't it, that they should keep insisting there was no sense in either bunch starting a real row with the other?" interpolated the sheriff.

"Not at all," Slade answered. "They didn't want a range war to break out that would very likely end with one faction or the other knocked out of business. They just wanted to keep each outfit suspicious and distrustful of the other and each blaming the other for whatever went wrong. Oh, they were smart operators, all right. Well, they're both dead and if you want to hold an inquest you can ride out to that cave and bring 'em in. I didn't feel exactly up to it."

"The devil with 'em!" growled Sloan.

"My sentiments," Slade agreed. "The few of their bunch left alive are scattered and on the run. I'll keep them in mind for future reference."

"What I can't understand," commented the sheriff, "is why nobody else ever discovered that water before now."

"Nothing remarkable about it," Slade pointed out. "In fact the really remarkable thing is that it was discovered at all. The rock formation is down at the bottom of that infernal sink, which anybody with the sense of a horned toad would avoid while crossing the desert. It would seem hard to find a more unlikely location for water. The mass of rock radiates heat like the breath of a blast furnace and that alone would cause a person to shy away from it. And you could ride within a couple of yards of the opening in the cliff without seeing it, the way the rock folds over. I'd say that location is just about the lowest and deadliest portion of the desert, but because it is the lowest and the closest to the underground water system is doubtless the explanation of how the cave comes to tap the subterranean stream. Perhaps Dawson learned about it from some old-timer who in turn learned it from the Indians, who appeared to know everything about the desert.

"Anyhow, he learned it somehow and put the knowledge to use in furthering his hell-raising. That cave will make a nice grave for him and his sidekick. The important thing is that they're both finished. Now maybe we can have peace hereabouts for a while."

Which was just what old Tom Wardell said when Slade reached the Flying W ranchhouse and told him everything that happened.

"I'm arranging a big barbecue and a get-together," old Tom added. "All the folks from over east are coming. You'll stay for it, won't you, son?"

Slade glanced teasingly at Dolores. "Well—reckon I could do worse," he agreed. "Then I'll have to be heading for the Post to see what else Captain Jim has lined up for me, but I'll be back."

"You'd better be," Dolores told him. Old Tom chuckled and looked pleased.

Two days later they watched him ride away, tall and graceful atop his great black horse, the rising sun etching his sternly handsome profile in flame.